Emily Brontë

More Myself Than I

a novel

by

John Passfield

Rock's Mills Press
Oakville, Ontario
2020

Published by
Rock's Mills Press
www.rocksmillspress.com

ISBN-13: 9778-1-77244-197-0

Cover Design: Craig Passfield

Cover Illustration: Emily Brontë: A Self-Sketch

Author's Website: www.johnpassfield.ca

For information, contact the publisher at customer.service@rocksmillspress.com.

Chapter 1

Emily 1

Sitting in the dining room. The clock has just gone nine. The cat is snug in Father's chair. Keeper is on the rug. Gondal is in abeyance for a while.

A pen moving firmly across a page.

Charlotte is sitting to the left of me. Anne is on my right. Branwell is gone to the Black Bull. Cathy is down at the farm-house gate. Heathcliff is under a cloak. At this moment, I am more myself than I.

To be

A girl who is aware of another existence.
Drops of blood on a broken pane of glass.
An old servant telling ancient tales.

a pack of dogs

Why the wish to write a novel?
What is the nature of a novel?
Just what does a novel do?

attacking an intruder.

A parsonage on a hill above a church.
Gaunt thorns all stretching one way.
A paper to be opened at a future time.

Running on the moors! As cold and fresh as I'll ever be! When the wind blows over the Heights, I feel most free!

Three sisters sitting in a room.

Father should be home soon. He said he would be home today. I waited by the gate what seems like all day. I should have stayed at my post. He might have arrived while I've been out here on the moors. A whip! A whip! A whip! A whip to whip the wind! I shall run as fast as I can to Wuthering Heights!

A boy lived in a parsonage. He had a brilliant mind. A brilliant future lay before him. A prodigy with paints and brushes. Someday the world would know what he could do.

"The solitary neighbour that I shall be troubled with."

Going for a walk – peeling potatoes. Setting the table – sitting in church. Two children – raised together – one an orphan – a waif – brought home by the father of the family, from Liverpool. How will I tell Heathcliff about Edgar Linton? He will never admit to the qualities which Edgar displays.

Different from other people - always be emily brontë - what is inside - as if through water - clock has just gone nine - the brontë four - search for sustenance - all manner of folk - break through this membrane - the perfect temperature.

Many times I have come to the window! I can only come at night! I am denied the sight of the crocuses and the melting snow!

A street rat in Liverpool
found himself without a home.

It's extremely cold in these parts. There are hardly any buildings. These people must turn to ice in the wintertime.
Pens and ink and paper on a table.
What does the old fellow want with me? A slave, no doubt, to do his bidding on the farm. He keeps asking me if I'm tired. Well I can walk further and faster than you, old man. You look like you're ready to drop. If you do I'll leave you here to freeze in the ditch. Not much further, he keeps on saying. I'll see what he wants with me. Can't be worse than the slums of Liverpool. If it isn't what I want, I'll run away.

A young girl lived in a parsonage. She was the eldest of three surviving sisters. They had a brother who was brilliant. They thought of themselves as the Brontë Four. They would write and paint for hours and hours each day.

Sitting at the dining room table.
Charlotte on my left and Anne on my right.

The poems didn't sell. Just as well – just as well. Like having the public pawing through one's drawers. Charlotte says the novels will sell. Readers enjoy an uplifting tale. My novel begins with a snowstorm out on the moors.

To prepare themselves - studied the master's secrets - hardly alive at all - communicate so seldom - told me so herself - cups of tea - I had a peep - a drawing of a girl - i'll be the grass - peace and harmony.

I have heard noises at the window many times! At times, I have even heard your voice! But never once, in all these years, have you appeared to me!

Mile after mile the two went on.
Man and boy on country roads.

What is this? What is this? What is this that Father has brought? It is nothing but a dirty little boy!
A dog asleep on a floor.
Why would he bring such a wretched thing home from Liverpool? Soaking wet and not a word. He doesn't seem to know how to talk. Another brother? – another tyrant! Hindley is brother-enough is what I say!

A boy who plans to stun the Royal Academy.
A young girl, motionless and mute.
A station exposed to atmospheric tumult.

Howarth parsonage serves the town. It is not a great metropolis. People go to larger towns on market days. We have lived here almost all our lives. It is the centre of our imaginary world.

Would you say that you will live in your characters?
Will your characters live in you?
Will your characters have a life unknown to you?

I enjoy going out on the moors. It's the highlight of my day. In any weather – it doesn't matter – me and my dog. The moors have been here since before time began. They'll be here, we can be sure, after it's gone.

A girl lived in a parsonage. She was the youngest of three surviving sisters. They had a brother who was brilliant. They thought of themselves as the Brontë Four. They would write and paint for hours and hours each day.

Wronged both thee and heaven \ and never care \ unknown eternity \ but only spirit \ the frightful dream \ subdued by passions \ win thee 'gainst thy will \ true to myself \ the world within \ its course of light.

Mumbled words in the depths of a cellar.
A centre hall-way with two main living rooms.
Cows being milked by light of a lantern.

It is early days with the novel. In some ways, it is all in my head; in some ways is it yet to be thought of. What comes next and what comes after is what we will see.

A beautiful country / extinguishing the light / minded little what tale was told / being repulsed continuously / heard her voice within / the concentrated essence / I couldn't conceive / more myself than i / earn honours by drawing blood / the fool's craving to hear.

What are these? Why do they stare? He kept telling me that I would be his son. He didn't tell me he had two brats of his own.
Wind making noises in the chimney.
They don't look very friendly. Am I to be a servant to these two? I smell food and the fire is warm. He'll probably lock me out in that barn. I don't think I'll like it here. The son is having a fit. The little girl just stares. I can't tell what to make of the little girl.

A girl lived in a parsonage.

I have not always been myself.
At times I have been someone else.
At times I have walked out on the moors.
At times I have sat down in this chair.

"Oh, wicked, wicked! May the Lord deliver us from evil!"

The novel is coming along quite well. For sure it wants to be written. What I know is what I know and what I don't know will soon be apparent. When the novel is done, I will show it to Charlotte. She will package it up with the others and send them away.

Never stand a chance - to blame me - reveal and conceal - think my private thoughts - a very simple plan - not her house - the familiar road - a chorus of selfishness - angels wonder - take in every word.

I've been a waif for twenty years! I've been wandering in the dark! I've been knocking at the window all this time!

They were wading in the beck.

Thinking silently of their dreams.

My whip! Where is my whip? Lost? How can it be lost? I especially asked for a whip from Liverpool!
A branch tapping lightly on a pane.
I need it for my pony! This little urchin has caused the loss! He has distracted Father's attention! He will be no brother of mine! Hindley is more than brother-enough! Our family is better left the way it is!

An old man brings a ragamuffin home from Liverpool.

Waiting with Cathy for her whip.
Huddling with Heathcliff under the cloak.

About to board the coach for London! Socks and cravats and toothpowder! So typical of the girls! I hardly listen as I allow my mind to expand! All I need are my paints and my bushes! I shall set London on its ear! I shall stun the Royal Academy! They shall not have seen my like! A portrait painter to the finest families of the realm! A townhouse in a fashionable esplanade! A coach-in-four for Sunday drives! My paintings hung – with those of Holbein and Reynolds – in ancestral halls! Members of Parliament! – Prime Ministers! No doubt, some day, a portrait of the Queen! Her growing family will keep me busy over the years! Receptions at court! Attendance at plays! Testimonials to all the other great men of the time! I pledge a toast to all and sundry! May the sun shine on you all as it has on me! Humble though my origins, I have reached the loftiest heights! The coach arrives! I spare a hug for my silly sisters! Your brother has soared above your heads! I shake the dust of Haworth from my feet!

A simple matter - keep us all at peace - living another life - walking for years and years - a little too much attention - birds and chicks - what are the words - shelter from a storm - what is blame - to release the jubilee.

Years of agony for me! I can almost hear you breathe! You haunt me but I never see your face!

Every day the lapwing would circle over the moors.
Every day she would search for sustenance.

Two snivelling brats! A broken fiddle and a lost whip! I'd be glad to break their heads! I'd like to see them scramble for scraps in Liverpool!
Tiny words hand-written on a page.
The mother don't want me. The servant turns up her nose. There is misery in this house. Why does the old man insist on keeping me? The fire is warm

and there's plenty of food. I'll stay a few days and then I'll run away.

"I came when the mistress was married, to wait on her; after she died, the master retained me for his housekeeper."

Oh there was once a shepherd lad.
He tended his sheep by day.
When the sun went down he led them home
and put them in the barn.

A mother who dies far too young.
A soul which was twinned at birth.
A kirk which is mouldering into ruin.

He fell asleep beneath a tree.
The sun had since gone down.
He dared not lead his sheep to home
and put them in the barn.

Of what is a novel made?
How will you ever find the words?
Is a novel born out in the world or somewhere inside?

There was Heathcliff and a girl at large.
The night was growing cold.
He wished that he was in the barn
asleep upon the hay.

The clock strikes and I am jerked back down to earth. Oh, I am sitting at the table. Charlotte is to the left of me. Anne is to my right. I put my pen down and roll my fingers over my eyelids.
The chimes of a clock on a landing.
Emily-Cathy – Emily-Heathcliff – Emily-Charlotte – Emily-Anne. At times like this, I am more myself than I. The other pens stop writing. We agree to exchange first lines. My only offering is a number – 1801.

Chapter 2

Cathy 1

Sweeping the carpet – sweeping the carpet. Charlotte is ironing in the kitchen. In the spring we take the carpets outside and drape them over the wall and set to task with the carpet-beater. Whack! – whack! – whack! – whack! – whack! Clouds and clouds of accumulated dust. Making the particles dance and sing. A great explosion – a concatenation – with every swing.

Two children running hand in hand.

Roaming on the moors. Completely wild and savage and free. I show Heathcliff the old woman's cave. Heathcliff shows me a lapwing's nest. *A pen and ink commentary.* When I take my pony along, he runs beside. Just the two of us alone. *Catherine Earnshaw – her book.* No Hindley to degrade Heathcliff. No Joseph to babble and shout. No Frances with her simpering chatter and pulling of hair. *An unformed childish hand.* Watching the clouds moving across the heavens. Feeling the rain come pouring down. *The unknown Catherine.* Never a thought for church or for schooling. Never a notion that we are both going straight to hell.

To be

A fang ripping into flesh.
A girl who calls herself an angel.
A clutch of grass growing out of rock.

a canary

How does a novel come to be made?
What do you gather in your basket?
What do you trample underfoot?

left out on the moors in winter.

An account book with all the pages filled.
Grass growing up between flagstones.
Sisters writing stories in a tiny hand.

An awful Sunday. I miss my father.
Two children sitting on a sack of corn.
Hindley is surely no substitute. He treats Heathcliff as my father would never do. Endless rain so we don't go to church. I like to watch the people there. At church one can consider all manner of folk. Some of them strut up the walk with their noses in the air. *All day had been flooding.* Heathcliff and I in the garret. Three hours on a sack of corn. Hindley and Frances basking in warmth at the fire downstairs. *Ranged in a row.* Joseph was born to condemn the heathen. He is very good at that. Three hours on the road to salvation – a cold and miserable path. Blistering tongue and accusatory eyes. *Groaning and shivering.* Climbing down, at last, from the garret. Hoping that Hindley won't play the tyrant and send us back.

One day he painted the family portrait. He called it the Brontë Four. Three sisters and their brother. He was brilliant as a painter. He would go to London Town and study art.

"Mr. Heathcliff and I are such a suitable pair to divide the desolation between us."

A boy is playing a fiddle! Amazing that he can play at the first try! A sound that I have never heard! It sounds very like a melody that a band of gypsies might play! A smile of contentment on his face as he plays his tune! A welcome to every soul with an open ear! We shall live as a band of gypsies! Gather our firewood in the forest! Dip our kettle in the flowing stream! Roast our supper on the fire as we dance and sing!

Nothing happens here - about a warning - dead woman who wonders - a secret from me - gondal is in abeyance - unknown eternity - scramble for scraps - the road to salvation - such a transgression - inside the novel.

I have been wandering the moors after midnight! Peeping in at windows and trying to see! But every window is a mirror that reflects itself back at me!
So I have never been able to see my loved ones! I have not seen Edgar, nor my daughter – yes I know there has been such a one – for lo these twenty years! Nor 'til tonight, my Heathcliff, have I been able to catch even a tiny glimpse of you!
I cannot go on from here! Not to heaven and not to hell! Until I know that all is well with those I have loved!

A street rat in Liverpool
learned to climb the castle wall.

Hindley demeaning Heathcliff. Encouraging Frances to pull his hair. The two of them taking the seats by the fire while we are both cold.
Two children staring at open books.
Joseph thrusts his books in our hands. Our hands are cold and the print is dingy. We turn away from the light of the fire to see the page. The heat of the fire is blocked by Hindley and his bride. If this is the way to heaven, who would want to live there at all? *Th' Helmet o' Salvation.* I glance at Heathcliff, who isn't reading – his eyes are fixed on me. I take the book by the scroop of the neck and fling it in among the dogs. They scramble out of the way so they won't have to read. Heathcliff drops his book on the floor and gives it a kick. *T' Brooad way to Destruction.* Joseph jumps up and commences to shouting. Hindley takes me by the collar and seizes Heathcliff by the arm, and drags us across the floor and through the door and slams it shut. *Think o' yer sowls.* We have been banished from the hearth. Joseph is shouting from the parlour. Fair flaysome that we both go on at this gate.

And so they spent a perfect childhood. Imagining stories and writing books. The boy and the eldest girl imagined an empire. The youngest girls imagined one as well. If only they could have lived in their minds alone.

Suffering indignities with Heathcliff.
Escaping and running loose on the moors.

Another boy begins to dance! Not a minuet nor a clog-dance nor a step-dance! Not at all like the dances we do at the parish fair! A dance that speaks of far-away places! Windy beaches and sunny skies! The two boys dance and play the fiddle as I clap my hands!

My eyes are blinded - write my story upon the flesh - what is the force - no significant people - blister their tender ears - make you merry - thorns reaching out - had no key - the imprints of fingers - i am the glue.

Heathcliff! I am in the grave all day! I am on the moors at night! How do we break through this membrane between us?
What did we do in life that was such a transgression? What have I done in death that keeps us apart? I have cried out to the elements – wind and rain, heaven and hell – to free us both so we can re-unite again!
I cannot get to heaven! I cannot approach the gates! I cannot find out what it is that has kept us apart!

It was harvest time
but bitter winds would blow.

Thrust by Hindley into the back kitchen. Only the remnants of a fire. *Two children slipping through a door.* The kind of cold that chills the marrow of the bones. Each of us seeks a place in a separate nook. *Sought a separate nook.* Time goes by and the clock ticks slowly. I read a book to pass the time – but Heathcliff doesn't read. I take a pen and ink and write of the day's events – but Heathcliff doesn't write. The time drags by and the clock is the only sound we hear. *The far-off fire.* Heathcliff leans over and whispers softly. Cathy! I have an idea! Let us go out and run in the rain! Let us scamper across the moors! We cannot be damper or colder than we are in here! *A dull ray.* Let us use the diary-woman's cloak to ward off the rain!

Flagstones with tufts of untrimmed grass.
A request for a short history.
A person reduced to his right place.

A steep street of cobblestones. Stationer, tavern, mason, tailor. Houses black with factory soot. Horses slipping – drivers climbing down to walk and lead. At the top a church and a graveyard – all one needs.

Are you the man with the whispering sickle?
Are you the girl who gathers the sheaves?
Are you the gleaner who scours the field when the harvest is done?

I start my day with chores. Peeling potatoes – that sort of thing. If there's to be meat, it must be purchased. And so I go out into the town. Occasionally, I buy paper at the stationer. Otherwise, I don't go into the town very much. I go the other way. I take the path and let myself out at the stile.

And so they spent a perfect childhood. Imagining stories and writing books. The boy and the eldest girl imagined an empire. The youngest girls imagined one as well. If only they could have lived in their minds alone.

Light my future sky \ all or half fulfil \ what is to be \ wakes one human heart \ shall be my dream \ weak and helpless prey \ pouring thy presence \ earth rising to heaven \ the sickened heart \ the hovering visions.

A chapel in a hollow between two hills.
An aging servant asking a girl to pillopatate.
Old guns and horse pistols above a chimney.

So completely removed / trust to my sagacity / bad feeling in the house / always be a good man / a rough-headed counterpart / the hazard of the lives / I oblige you to listen / neither am I aware / ached with some great grief / all the madness in the world.

Performing a ceremony in the churchyard – Heathcliff and I! Conjuring up a whole army of ghosts! A host of ghosts, I say, and Heathcliff laughs!

Two children dancing in a graveyard.

Come out! Come out! We dare you! Come and haunt us for all of our lives! All the Haretons and the Heathcliffs! All you people who used to live! How did you used to live in this kingdom? *How little did I dream.* What do you think about now you are dead? Do you flit around in the darkness? Visit the places you used to inhabit? Watch the people who live there now? Do you take a peek in at the windows and envy us? *Calls him a vagabond.* Do you wish you could live your life over? Run as free as Heathcliff and me? Take the dairy-woman's cloak and run through the rain on the moors? *Turn him out of the house.* Why don't you speak to us? We are listening! – truly listening! There must be much that we could learn! What lesson would you impart to our eager ears? Oh, what good to be a ghost if all you do is stay indoors? *He will reduce him.* Come out, come out, and haunt us! What did you learn while you were alive? We are waiting to hear what all of you have to say!

Her mother, her aunt and two elder sisters were dead.

At times I have been no one.
At times I have been everyone.
At times I have been this dog.
At times I have been this chair.

"Hey, Gnasher! Hey, dog! Hey Wolf, holld him, holld him!"

I take my whip and snap the air! There is a crackle like pine in a fire! I can feel the flames leap up as they notice me! I want you both to go faster! I snap my whip at the boy who plays the fiddle! – he fiddles for all he's worth! I snap my whip at the dancing boy! – he speeds up to the fiddle's pace! "Dance! – Play! Dance! – Play!" I shout as I crack my whip! The flames of the dancing fire caress my face!

Faded hieroglyphics - stoop to such baseness - the ideal emily-form - for me alone - keeper knew - turn and walk away - a man who makes plans - trampled all my magnanimity - so easily forgotten - fond, fond, fond.

I will spend anywhere with you! Whether on earth or in heaven or hell! All I wish for is to spend eternity with you!

I am looking at the window! It is a mirror – not a glass! I can see the day you first appeared to me!

There is so much I want to ask of you! I know that I gave birth! My lost child was a daughter, was she not?

He put his chest against the flow to hold it back.
She splashed and giggled in the water as it flowed.

Shall we go there and look in the window? We are not far from Thrush-cross Grange.

Two children walking along a path.

There are aristocrats dwelling there. We see them sometimes in church. They always turn up their noses as they walk up the path. What do you say Heathcliff? – what do you say? *Escaped from the wash-house.* They would never even know that we are there. Just two ghosts looking in on the human scene. *A ramble at liberty.* Oh, how do you think they live, Heathcliff? Silver platters and golden goblets? An army of servants to tie their shoes? Sugared sweets if they learn their lessons? Every breakfast a regal banquet? Do they drink each other's health with a glass of champagne? *A glimpse of the Grange lights.* Perhaps kings and queens would come to the Grange and visit from time to time. Carriages dripping with sparkling jewels and horses with plumes upon their heads, all prancing in step as the carriage moves up the drive. *Burning their eyes out.* The little girl always wears such marvelous clothes.

The young master hates the young ragamuffin as an intruder.

Spying in the window at Thrushcross Grange.
Falling asleep and awakening in a dream.

It is extremely dark! There is no moon tonight! The current is much faster than I thought it would be! I call up to the boat, but no one answers! I have nowhere to stay tonight, so I must get aboard! The man who rowed me out here keeps asking for his money! Are all Londoners so impatient? I call up towards the deck once again! "Who calls?" a gruff voice answers! "It is I! – Miss Brontë! – One of your passengers! I have purchased a ticket for France!" The current nudges the side of the rowboat and I almost fall down! "We sail tomorrow!" the voice calls back! "Come back tomorrow and we'll take you aboard!" "But I have nowhere to stay!" I call up to the voice! The voice does not answer! "I know no one here in London! – I do not come from these parts! – I can show you my ticket if you shine a lantern down!" "I can't let anyone come aboard!" calls the voice! The man who brought me out here wants his money so he can leave! Why would they not put out some lanterns? It is dark out here on the Thames! The rowboat is rocking from the wash of another boat! "I demand that you take me aboard!" The rushing current is threatening to sweep me away!

Make my escape - my breath on your cheek - broken a fingernail - spoke so beautifully of heaven - locked out in the cold - died inside my being - what did you see - hands are never clean - minds of a single thought - living a separate story.

I have lived at the brink of a membrane! I could sense you reaching out to me in your anguish and your grief! There were times I was almost able to speak to you!

I felt your breath as if I were living! Or you were dead and walking with me! I could almost feel we were cheek to cheek, but I could not see!

And now here I am at the window! Meet me, Heathcliff, on the heath! We shall talk and talk as we never did before!

Every day the lapwing would circle over the moors.
She would feed her little fledglings in her nest.

Looking in at the window. So this is Thrushcross Grange. Heathcliff and I standing tall on a flower pot.
Two children looking in a window.
A white ceiling with a golden border. A host of candles on a chandelier. The two young aristocrats whom we see on Sundays at church. How silly of them to be fighting over a tiny little dog. *From the top of the Heights.* Suddenly, there is barking! We turn and look but all is dark! Yelping and growling and people shouting as we turn and jump and run! Oh my ankle is seized and I fall and roll on the grass! *Beaten in the race.* A great beast has my ankle firm in its jaws! The pain is ferocious! – I am afraid! – Heathcliff is beating it with a rock! *Her shoes in the bog.* Everyone shouting and crowding around! The dog lets go and I roll over! I try to get up and walk! The pain is so intense that I feel I will faint! Someone seizes me and lifts me up and carries me away! *Groped our way up.* My head is bouncing against his arm! All I can feel is ferocious pain! *The light came from thence.* I cannot think or see. My head sags and all goes completely dark.

"He has nobody knows what money and every year it increases. Yes, yes – he's rich enough to live in a finer house than this."

A man lay down his head.
On a pillow his head he lay.
He tried to read an ancient book.
He read by candlelight.

A man who rejects his own children.

A dog seizing hold of a girl's ankle.
A daughter of a daughter and a son of a son.

The printed ink was faded.
The pages dark and old.
A girl had scribbled half her thoughts.
She wondered what to do.

Are you the blacksmith, the forge or the iron?
Are you the bird or the nest or the eggs?
Are you the maker or are you the thing that is being made?

Oh that was twenty years ago.
What now the questions be?
She knocks upon the window.
To ask what he would know.

Awakening in a palace. I am in London and I am the Queen.
A young girl in a palace safe and warm.
I blink my eyes and blink again. Many candles in a crystal chandelier. A great white bandage around my foot. It throbs with pain, but what of that? *A splendid place.* I am reclining like a princess upon a divan. A crowd of faces – a mother and a father – a young boy and a little girl. The many candles lend each face a welcome glow. *Carpeted with crimson.* Velvet drapes and a pure white ceiling and a border around the top. A golden border running all around the room. *A shower of glass drops.* Oh where is my Heathcliff? Where has he gone? Why has he not come in as well? He would enjoy the crimson and the velvet. He would marvel at the chandelier. *Hanging in silver chains.* The sea of faces closes in. Someone proffers a plateful of cakes. Served on a silver salver, as to the daughter of a king and a queen. *Running red-hot needles.* Oh Heathcliff we are both rescued! I shall ask these people to invite him in. I shall entice him to take a little sip of champagne.

Chapter 3

Heathcliff 1

Baking all through the day. Kneading the dough to the proper feel. Coaxing the fire to the perfect temperature. Arms all covered in flour. A brief respite with a cup of steaming tea. The cleanup and the meals. Heavy rain today. A shorter walk than usual, but bracing still. Nine o'clock and back inside the novel again.

A boy and a girl holding hands.

Cathy and me out on the moors. Running free and meeting no one. All the world as ours to explore. Not a Hindley, not a Joseph, not an emperor or a king. Not a one to make us read or muck out the stalls. *Order Heathcliff a flogging.* Cathy and I in total silence. We run – we laugh – we play. We don't have any secrets – we don't need any talk. No one to order us about. We never tell each other what to do. *Run away to the moors.* Wading and laughing in a little pool in the beck. Not a thought and not a care. *Discover them nowhere.* Taking her pony out on the moor-side. She rides like the wind and I run alongside. *They were invisible.* Showing Cathy a lapwing's nest. Cathy showing me a cave. Losing Cathy's shoe in a bog. It is times like these that make the rest worthwhile.

A key

A beck which flows past two troubled houses.
A voice crying out in the pouring rain.
A man who gives his wife a choice.

thrown into

Does Keeper ever dream?

Why does he whimper in his sleep?

Why do his legs twitch as if he is running across the moors?

a roaring fire.

Four children chatting as they paint.
A coal-shed, a pump and a pigeon-cot.
A mother who died while still quite young.

Sunday at the heights. A dreadful day for her – just another day for me. A price that is the price I pay each day.

A girl and boy escaping from a garret.

Hindley and Joseph are beasts from hell. They don't fool me with their pious words. *Do him an ill-turn.* Sitting here and thinking. Cathy is writing in a book. Might as well pour the ink on the floor. I had rather be bringing in hay or chopping wood. *Pride and black tempers.* Sitting and thinking of the future. Joseph grovelling and pleading for mercy. A paintbrush dripping with Hindley's blood. The whole facade of Wuthering Heights a crimson shade. *Against Heathcliff and Catherine.* There is so little heat from the fireplace. We would be warmer if we were in hell. What is the point of staying in here? We could slip out the back-kitchen door. We could run and play on the moors til the cows come home. *Heaping the heaviest blame.* I lean over and whisper to Cathy. We can take the milkmaid's cloak. Put that silly book away and let us go.

All the Brontës had some talent. All the Brontës could paint and draw. All the Brontës wrote poems and stories. But there was only one Brontë son. It was he who would carry their banner out into the world.

"I felt interested in a man who seemed more exaggeratedly reserved than myself."

I am little more than an infant! I am bending at my oar! From time to time I feel a lash across my back! I am charged with rowing this galley against the wind! We are making little headway! I am exhausted from the miles I have rowed! I let my oar loose and rub my arms to ease the pain! The sweat runs down my brow! My muscles quiver from fatigue! A sting of the whip and my back is assaulted with blinding pain!

A moment's thought - pull open every gate - it wasn't me - die of their neglect - at this moment - true to myself - stay a few days - the family portrait - cried out to the elements - all the world as ours.

Cathy! I have felt your presence as on the other side of a mirror! I have felt your breath on my cheek! What is this barrier that is keeping we two apart?

I have lived my life in agony! Crushed every rock and flower that has stood in my path! Every drop of blood in my body yearns for you!

I have battered at the gates of hell! I have demanded a list of the rules! Why is the gate so firmly chained which keeps us apart?

A street rat in Liverpool
made a nest beneath the throne.

We are dancing on the graves. All these people used to live. *A girl and boy dancing in a churchyard.* Cathy is teaching me to waltz. We bow to the honoured ghosts. Would any of you care to come out and dance? Would you care for a sip of champagne or some caviar? *She had ways with her.* Catherine says the aristocrats are all buried inside. We walk on them every Sunday. They look up at our muddy boots from their cold dark graves. *At high-water mark.* Who cares what they learned while they were alive? They were above us – now they are below us. *Singing, laughing and plaguing.* What good do your rings and jewels and cravats do you down there? Still holding the whip that you used to use on your slaves? I could dig you up and spit on you but I wouldn't waste the time. Cathy and me are both alive! – and you are dead! *The bonniest eye, the sweetest smile.* Breaking away and running free. Leaving the churchyard ghosts behind. On the moors there are no ghosts – just Cathy and me. Why would we want to have truck with ghosts? We only want to be left alone. There is no one living or dead that I want to see. *Lightest foot in the parish.* There is one or two, perhaps, that I wouldn't mind sending straight to hell. That day would be a pleasant day for me.

But time moved on and they all grew older. The brilliant brother went out into the world. Their father was aging – their father was ill. He was the sole support of the girls. Would it not be wise to prepare themselves for the world?

Running free on the moors.
Tagging along with Cathy to Thrushcross Grange.

A very large muscular man is glaring down at me! He is standing on the deck! My eyes are blinded by the glare as the sun beats down! He applies his lash with no mercy for lesser beings! I grit my teeth and pull my oar! A rain of lashes assaults my back! Despite the pain – I manage to dream my dream! Some day I will be much older! I will snap these hated chains! I will break this oar in two! I will seize the galley-master and throw him overboard! He will beg for mercy as he gurgles in the drink! I will laugh as he cries like a baby! What do I care that he cannot swim? His wife and children will wait in vain for their master to come home!

To dream my dream - I despised you - shattered the rock - what are the ingredients - leading a false life - what is the colour - music does not play - what i want - two children whispering - we shall have unity.

I heard your voice at the window! I thrust the fool aside! I saw your blood on the sill!

My face is pressed against the glass! I can hear you but I cannot see you! I cannot die with my life uncompleted!

I am calling out to you, Cathy! You are all I shall ever have! For all these years I have been desperate to speak with you!

"A better place than you've ever been.
A better place than you'll ever be."

Go to Thrushcross Grange? Go to Thrushcross Grange? Why in the world would we want to go to Thrushcross Grange?

A girl and boy walking along a path.

We have escaped one house of misery. Why would we want to approach another? *Forgot everything.* Aristocrats? Aristocrats? – the local magistrate, you mean! The man would cut off your arm if you stole an apple or two! Joseph says he keeps a gibbet in his orchard for boys like me. *They were together.* Oh we have seen them so often at church. Noses poking up in the air. How many times have we laughed and done the same? We turn our noses up at the sheep as we walk our way home. *The unfriended creatures.* Who would want to live in the home of a magistrate? He would punish you for every little thing you do. *Heathcliff by himself.* Oh, who cares how they live? Their minds are as starched as their clothes. I would rather muck out the stable than drink their champagne.

A girl dressed in white near an open window.
An intruder who asks for a guide.
A person who will never have a comfortable home.

Haworth tavern – the Black Bull. Disrespectful people are often known to frequent its dens. Within a walk – or a crawl – of the parsonage.

Does Keeper have nightmares too?
Could he dip his paw in ink and write a book?
How deep or how shallow would such a book tend to be?

Anne and I write Gondal poems and stories, but Anne less so as time has gone by. Gondal means something different to the both of us, I would say. Which characters are me I wouldn't care to consider. They are, all of them, inside me – somewhere at large.

But time moved on and they all grew older. The brilliant brother went out in the world. Their father was aging – their father was ill. He was the sole support of the girls. Would it not be wise to prepare themselves for the world?

I've seen those forms \ no promised heaven \ hope's spell \ true to myself \ the blasted sorrow \ the hostile light \ lost to mortality \ heaven descending \ i am born to bear \ tomorrow wake.

Narrow windows deep-set in a wall.
Moorlands stretching for miles and miles.
A house with large, jutting cornerstones.

The stir of society / lost in the marshes / alone in the world / not a minute's security / confident, innocent angels / gone through and through me / the honeysuckles embracing the thorn / I'll swallow the key / worried myself to discover.

I'm soaking wet to the core. So is Cathy too. We got lost in the bog. We lost her shoe somewhere in the dark. Go and get it when things dry out. There is run-off dripping down on this flowerpot.
Two children looking through a pane.
Looking in at the window. All the fancy things inside. Crimson carpets – crimson chairs. Crimson all around the room. As if they have draped great velvet curtains inside a barn. *A ramble at liberty.* I bet they never go run on the moors. The rain would damage their velvet clothes. A drop of rain and they would both be kept inside. *A glimpse of the Grange lights.* A pure white ceiling, bordered by gold. Glass drops hanging from silver chains. A pretty penny spent for tapers to light the room. *Shoes in the bog.* Fighting over a pile of fur. Cathy and me would never fight. I never envy her nor does Cathy envy me. Whatever I have is hers and hers is mine. *Burning their eyes out.* They have no idea we are here. We can watch everything they do. Almost like looking down at the ants from far above. *Clinging to the ledge.* We make fun of them every Sunday. Cathy and me has got each other. We have everything we want. We don't need any fancy buckles on our shoes.

Her father, brother and two sisters were still alive.

At times I have been a prisoner.
At times I have owned the goal.
At times I have walked in wildflowers.
At times I have walked through hell.

"It's fair flaysome that ye let 'em go on this gait. Ech! th' owd man wad ha' laced 'em properly – but he's goan!"

Some day I will be a master! I will stand on the deck and sneer! I will wield my master's lash! Then the galley-slaves will have to answer to me! I will have bided my time in silence! I will have studied the master's secrets – learned the art of inflicting pain! These slaves will know my anger! I will make the lashes sting! I shall write my story upon the flesh of their backs! Every scar will be my testament! I shall stand astride the deck – shouting for ever and ever more speed! When their eyes roll up to the heavens they will only see me!

A line of upright stones - speaking on my behalf - the best that is you - what i have in common - other pressing things - look down his nose - never see eye to eye - the mud of your own concerns - living books and dying people - avoid my storms.

You held the key away from your husband! He tried to wrest it from your hand! I despised you for what you had caused your life to be!

You despised him that he was not me! If you knew not that, then you did not know yourself! You had thrown yourself into a bog and could not get out!

I could have thrashed him into jelly! I could have reduced him to a blubbering child! When I turned to you, he struck me on the throat!

"I wonder where it goes?" she said.
"It goes not anywhere!"

The jaws of hell! – the jaws of hell! The dog has Cathy in its grip! It has fastened itself to her ankle and won't let go!

A boy smashing a stone against a skull.

I grab a stone and smash its skull! It try to pry apart its jaws! I try to force the stone between its slavering lips! The devil hangs on and shakes its head! *Running hot needles.* I smash my head against its head! I bite its nose as hard as I can! I poke my fingers in its eyes and rake my claws! The beast has Cathy in its jaws and won't let go! *Shot like arrows.* The snorting and slavering of the dog! – Cathy crying for me to go! I curse the dog and smash my fist against its skull! *Spitted on the horns.* Shouting – feet on gravel – a jerking lantern! I am torn away from the dog! Cathy's foot a mass of skin and slaver and blood!

The young girl loves the ragamuffin as she loves herself.

Fighting off a slavering dog.
Watching Princess Cathy through the thick glass panes.

A position of my own. My very first venture out into the world. A chance to earn my own way and contribute to the family my proper share. I am sure that I must be more assertive than heretofore I have been. A balance of kindness and of firmness will be best to cultivate as an ideal. I must overcome my shyness – I barely talk to the butcher-boy when he calls, or to the stationer in the shop, or to those who make their pleasantries at church – but I shall make much more of an effort to assert myself when called upon to do so; but only as befitting my situation, of course. A governess – a governess – a chance to inculcate and influence. Preparation – preparation – making a list and checking again. What I shall wear – what I shall pack – what I shall wash and iron and fold. Travel arrangements have all been secured. In a few days I shall be venturing out into the to-and-fro of the world – as governess to the children of Blake Hall.

Buried deep in fallen snow - unable to break through - see heathcliff as his twin - only you and me - clutching the key - never reach heaven nor hell - what have you heard - the air swarmed - a man obsessed by images - see it as a vantage point.

Deep in the ground or high in the sky! Inside the gates of hell or camped on the hillside outside the walls! What would it matter if you and I were together again?

I go to the window night after night! I feel your presence but I do not see your face! I see scenes that I have lived through – but they are blurred as if looking through ice!

Let us not talk of other people! Other people are agony to me! All of our troubles were due to the people who clogged our path!

One day the lapwing circled over the moors.
She returned to find a trap set over her nest.

I follow them into the house! I swear and curse at these fiends and their dog! How dare you sic your dog on a little girl! *A boy being flung by ruffians onto a lawn.* Cathy is lying on the velvet bench. She is sick with such terrible pain. The idiots crowd around and stare. They keep talking as if we are thieves. They think she was trying to steal their stupid chandelier. *Out-and-outer.* I curse and curse and curse and curse! How dare you talk that way of her! Get a doctor for her foot! See how she bleeds! *Foul-mouthed thief.* A fellow grabs me by the shoulders! I try to twist away! *Go to the gallows.* Cathy revives but there is terrible pain in her face! No! We must never be apart! If she is here then I am here! *Fasten the chain.* He thrusts me through the doorway! You cannot send me from this house! We are together – you don't understand! He wrestles me outside! *Frightful thing.* He drags me into the garden and throws me to the ground! Be off with you before we loose the dogs!

"Rough as a saw-edge, and hard as whinstone! The less you meddle with him the better."

A lady in the window.
A book upon the sill.
The light wind lifts the pages.
No pages readeth she.

A pilgrim's staff used as a cudgel.
A voice crying out in the pouring rain.
A distraught man bashing his head against a tree.

She wears the white of angels.
She feels a kick within.
She gazes out the window.
To see what she can see.

Is Keeper as tormented as you seem to be?
Is he exploring unknown worlds?
Is he questioning how the universe is made?

A movement in the garden.
A shadow lurks below.
Her hair is shorn with scissors.
She wonders where she's been.

Watching Cathy through the window. Like a queen on her divan. *A boy walking home alone in the dark.* All the courtiers ranged around her. Giving her sweets on silver pans. She is beautiful in the candle-light. *Their great glass panes.* Buy her a dozen chandeliers. Bring her champagne in golden goblets to slake her thirst. *As merry as could be.* All the starched ones crowd around her. She is a million times better than they. *Stupid admiration.* They have forgotten me out here. Only the darkness and the crickets. The dogs, for now, have been put away. *Immeasurably superior.* Watching Cathy through the window. A long walk back to the Heights. What is waiting for me there? Dark as hades – not even a star. *Everybody on earth.* Her shoe is stuck somewhere in the bog. Better for me if I should throw myself in as well.

Chapter 4

Cathy 2

The day's events have ended. The rain came down in torrents. We almost didn't walk. Anne lost a shoe as we walked along. A blast of soot from the fireplace. A mop and water clears us of this deed. Now ink and pen and paper. There will be chores another day. I take this ball and kneed this muddy clay.

A snarling dog at the entrance to a faery cave.

We are attending the royal carriage. It is rumbling up the drive. Hindley and I are the two outriders. We are accompanying the royals from church. *A prince in disguise.* Oh Heathcliff! Heathcliff! Heathcliff! This is good news for us both! *Emperor of China.* I slide down from my horse and open the carriage door. Isabella descends from the carriage. I hold her hand as a servant would. Hindley takes her arm and leads her into the Heights. *An Indian queen.* Edgar takes a look around him. He remains in the carriage door. He hesitates to put his foot on the ground. *High notions of my birth.* Mother warned of that dreadful boy. Is he anywhere around? Mother wonders why your brother keeps him here. *Smothered in cloaks and furs.* I assure him that all is safe and we go inside.

To be

A boy who is kidnaped by pirates.
A girl who wastes away and dies.
Hot coffee after a bone-chilling walk.

a person

Why communicate so seldom with other people?

Can one live a life with no significant people at all?
What are the ingredients of an Emily-Brontë day?

who is searching for lost years.

Sitting and listening to the sermon in the church.
An old man's pocket full of apples and pears.
A girl with the eyes of a half-tamed creature.

Oh, it is Heathcliff! – wonderful Heathcliff! Come to welcome us to the house!

A boy shaking hands with himself in the glass.

Nelly has made him much more than decent. Face all scrubbed and hair all combed. No sullen, dirty scruff of a farm-boy now. *Dress you smart.* Ellen has worked some measure of magic. She is surely a witch in disguise. No more wrinkles on his forehead – no more devils darken his eyes. They sparkle in friendship, like two bright angels. *Make me decent.* I hold out my hand and bring him forward. I turn to Edgar and Isabella. May I present my friend at court? *Going to be good.* It is Heathcliff – a whole new Heathcliff. Broad in the shoulders – brimming with health. *Converted into a stranger.* Who now should bow to whom, Edgar? Who now should look up to whom? *Chance of being as rich.* It is Heathcliff – wonderful Heathcliff! A prince, you must agree! All along he has been a prince, though well disguised!

One day he took the coach to London. His sisters saw him off. He packed his paints and brushes. He packed some samples of his work. Before too long the brilliant boy came walking home.

"Mr. Heathcliff offers a singular contrast to his abode and style of living."

I am going to write a book! A book about myself! I am snug inside my oak dresser! No one can see me here! The pine cones scratch at the window! The cold wind howls outside! What has happened to me so far! What I will cause to happen next! The path of my life I will trace with my ink and my pen!

Worlds of light - in separate worlds - would it matter to you - three people standing - aware of another existence - the world within - twinned at birth - divide the desolation - to free us both - in total silence.

Lately something has happened to me – like having glimpses of what is to be! A little boy was herding some sheep – I know I saw him and I am sure he saw me! But the moment was so brief I could hardly believe!

And this moment, here, at the window! I could see that gentleman inside! I could see right through the window – in a way that I am unable to see you now!

No, my hand is no longer bleeding! I'm sure the gentleman meant no harm! He didn't understand that I thought that he was you!

A street rat in Liverpool
snuggled up beside the king.

They are attacking my Heathcliff mercilessly! Hindley is shoving him towards the kitchen! Saying things that sting my soul!.
A prince and a plough-boy in disguise.
Keep the plough-boy out of sight, Ellen. His boots are as muddy as his soul. He'll be wiping his hands on the tablecloth – sticking his fingers into the fruit. *Keep the fellow out.* So this is your work, is it Ellen? Dressing a devil in Sunday attire? *Send him into the garret.* Fling the devil into the stable. Lock him up in the garret til night. He can come out when all the decent folk have gone home. *Begone you vagabond.* I won't forget this treachery, Nelly. I'm so mad I could pull his hair out by the roots. *Like a colt's mane.* Edgar begins to attack him as well. Oh his hair looks that of a sheepdog. I wonder that he has the use of his eyes. Edgar barely finishes his insult when a tureen of hot apple sauce is overturned on his face and fancy clothes. Like lightning, Hindley snatches up Heathcliff by the scruff of the neck and escorts him brutally out of the room. *Heathcliff's violent nature.* My faery-tale is covered in muck before my eyes.

She cast around for a means of livelihood. A number of schemes were put into practice. All three sisters tried and failed. As teachers of girls who had no interest. As governesses to ungrateful children. They published a book of poems that never sold.

Surprised to see Heathcliff made so decent.
Grateful to Ellen for making him so.

I have an ink-pot and a pen! No one saw me as I took them from the table! But I have no paper to write on! No paper here but what someone has already used! I have plenty of books in the windowsill! Sometimes they block the light! I have perused them many times and tossed them aside! Where is my book with a sheaf of blank pages! I too have a tale to begin! I too have a story to make! If all these writers are allowed to write then why not I?

Snap these hated chains - did not know yourself - caused a storm - sting my soul - thought and wonder - cut out his tongue - a throbbing membrane - not fulfil the promise - see in the shifting flames - much has been altered.

I too have not lived! I spent all those years upon this earth! – as a daughter and a wife! And yet I feel that I was hardly alive at all!

Only when we were out on the heath! Not at home – at Wuthering Heights! Not in the graveyard, dancing on the graves! – not beneath the chandeliers at Thrushcross Grange!

Oh what is the force, my Heathcliff? What is the force that drove us apart? What was it that shattered the rock beneath our feet!

"If you're for riding,
sure the whip is for my daughter.

This is Edgar – silly Edgar! He has caused a storm in our house! Now he stands there blubbering and wiping his fancy clothes! *A girl with strange welts on her back.* Oh why did you speak to him in that manner? Now Hindley is making a row! He shall be flogged and I cannot stand it! *Snatched up the culprit.* I feel pain with every blow! You should never have spoken to Heathcliff in that way! He held out his hand in friendship! He welcomed you to the house! *A rough remedy.* He wipes his brow with his fancy handkerchief – his aristocratic handkerchief. He looks so silly, I want to laugh. *It served him right.* I didn't! Oh I didn't! I didn't speak at all! I told Mama I wouldn't speak to him, and I never spoke one word! I am surprised that you speak to me in that manner at all! *Weeping to go home.* Are you dead? Are you wounded? Are there welts across your back? Don't speak of him to Hindley or Hindley will want to flog him more! *In a bad temper.* Oh now you've upset Isabella! Let us put this out of mind. You are not damaged, are you, Isabella? So what can be your excuse? *Spoilt your visit.* Let us sit down and continue the occasion. Let us go on as if this had never happened at all.

A sea-storm subsiding magically.
A snail shrinking icily into itself.
A person with a private manner of interpreting.

The moors sweep right up behind the house. An iron turnstile, a meadow with quarry pits, another iron turnstile and one is right out on the moors. Moorcock, lapwing, eagle – fern and furze. A clear cold wind coming down off the hills.

Do you see yourself as in prison?
Do you yearn to run free on the moors?
If not as is, what would you like to do and to be?

I always date my poems. I write the day, the month and the year. That, I suppose, is my anchor. The rest is sailing or – perhaps – flight. I keep them private, my poems. There are people who like to pry. I don't write for other people – I write for me. Do you know music, at all? Are you that way inclined?

The poems are the imagery of my life, in a different key.

She cast around for a means of livelihood. A number of schemes were put into practice. All three sisters tried and failed. As teachers of girls who had no interest. As governesses to ungrateful children. They published a book of poems that never sold.

Live in eternal spring \ no threatened hell \ my maturer eyes \ my own wild will \ sense of utter woe \ this quenchless will \ does not warm but burn \ took my heart to me \ a reckless course \ makes me strong.

A cold and misty afternoon.
A letter with a reference to a second book.
A chair, a clothes-press and a large oak case.

The atmospheric tumult / suffer no resurrection / had some ups and downs / through wind and rain / more in themselves and less in surface / thwarting his own revenge / whatever our souls are made of / was not the chief consideration / I related the scene / a stranger, an exile, an outcast.

Hindley is beating Heathcliff mercilessly! I am feeling every blow! Edgar speaks to me but I do not hear his voice!
A group of people making small-talk over tea.
I smile, perhaps grimly, but he takes it as his due. Isabella chirps in too and I force a smile. *Should not have spoken.* Oh, a blow across my back! I can feel the pain in my ribs! I shall have Heathcliff's welts on my back tomorrow, I know! *Hate him to be flogged!* My ribs have often been painful. Heathcliff thinks Hindley broke one of his ribs – last week when Hindley struck him a vicious blow. I feel blood trickling down my forehead! Hindley is beating him with a club! *Can't eat my dinner.* What is that? Pray, what do you say? Yes, the weather will surely clear. Yes Edgar, I quite agree. I would love to walk in the park next sunny day. *Why did you speak.* Isabella, I'm sure, would enjoy such an outing too. Hindley returns to us at the table and the party resumes.

She had a dog and a pet bird.

I have been everyone in Haworth.
I have been everyone in this house.
I have been warmed by this fire
and burned by this fire as well.

"Und haw is't that nowt comed in frough' th' field, be this time? What is he abaht? girt eedle seeght!'

Very well then! – very well! I shall write my book in the pages of other books! I will make my mark on everyone else's marks! I have no care for what they have written! What have they to do with me? I take down a dusty old tome and open the page! I dip my pen in the ink and I start to write! I write the story that I want to record! I write at the bottom – I write at the top – I write on the margins on both sides! I turn the pages on their sides and write over-top of the printed words! Let the wind howl – I don't care to listen! Let the pine cones scratch at the window! My story is mine and only mine! Now all of these pages belong to me! All of these books are mine alone! No one will ever know what I have written inside!

A child once more - a moral poison - you will be less - particular to myself - look upon her face - a backbone or a fist - not her natural home - the faded vision - the teller of all the tales - enjoy my sunny days.

Degrade me to marry you? Degrade me to marry you? How could I have said those words?

There was a madness took ahold! It sometimes pulled me either which way, by an arm! I had no idea what I was saying at such a time!

No, I did not move on – I did not move down the road and leave you behind! I was with you all along! You were in my head and my heart – we shared one soul!

"Let us hold the water back," he said,
As it flowed around his chest.

The dinner party trundles on its remorseless way. Hindley regales us with the details. I have given that clod a thrashing to within a thin inch of his life. *A girl who asked for a whip that never came.* And you, young Master Edgar, if he ever insults you again, or even looks at you askance and you take it as an insult, why give a workout to your fists, and you shall feel the better for it. Give the devil his due is what I always say. *Wouldn't say one word.* Well the goose is a pleasure, Ellen. You have done that well, at least. I shall do my duty, in turn, with this carving knife. *You're not killed.* I have locked him in the garret where he can think about remorse. But the scriptures tell us the devil cannot repent. I gave orders to Ellen to let the villain starve. *Make more mischief.* My Heathcliff lies aching in the garret! I feel every welt on his back! He groans and rolls himself over to ease the pain! *Brute of a lad.* Hindley serves each plate in turn. I say a servant is a servant and a master is a master and the servant should be grateful to be put in his place. There are servants who need a regular letting of blood. *Your own fists.* I am about to burst into tears. I drop my fork and pretend to fetch it to hide my face. *No real harm.* We drink our toast to family. I almost choke on mine. The dinner drags on and on. Idle chatter – idle minds. *Carved bountiful platefuls.* The tyrant at his table. The Lintons seem impressed. I sit and sip and chatter. *Merry with lively talk.* My heart is in the garret. Oh when will this purgatory end?

The two young children run and scamper on the moors.

Suffering with Heathcliff as he is thrashed.
Rescuing Heathcliff from his exile.

Rain and mud! Mud and rain! Dreary landscape! Weary day! Riding on the coach! Riding outside for lack of funds! If the pennies run out I will have to walk in this mire for miles and miles! A miserable failure of a journey! Bespattered with mud and grime! London was terrifyingly large! Rattling wheels and plunging horses! Every intersection a tangle of curses and fists! What will I tell the others? Charlotte will have nothing for me but contempt! She is counting on me to earn the daily bread! She will mention Holbein and Reynolds! She will hiss them in my face! She will ask if the Duke of Wellington sat for me! Rather face Anne or even Emily if I had my choice! Wheels squealing! – horses neighing! Hope we don't have to get out and walk! My head is reeling faster than one of these muddy wheels! I stink like no-one's business! Lost my money! Lost my gloves! Spattered in mud from top to toe! Drinking and drunk is all I remember! And being ejected out into the street! A terrifying night of torrential rain! My mind whirls round and round! Did I ever show my drawings? Did I ever present my card? Did I ever even go to the College of Art?

One figure erased - managed to reach beyond - that is my key - you did not see - lurking here in the garden - like the ghosts you conjured - the lapwings were a distraction - to repair some of his wrongs - choose to call his soul - to release the birds.

I thought that my rock was you, but you withdrew yourself from me – as I in my terrible nightmare withdrew from you! Is that force still extant now? – will we be thwarted beyond the grave?
Is it enough to want to be one? For me to be you and for you to be me? Do we get to choose the parameters of our soul?
Oh meet me tonight at the churchyard! We are the strongest humans I know! If anyone can decide on eternity, it shall be we!

Every day the lapwing would circle over her nest.
The fledglings were starving for the sustenance she held in her beak.

In the evening we have our dance. People come from the countryside. I beg Hindley to let Heathcliff go.
A dance for almost everyone in the parish.
Oh please – let him come down! There is every person here, of every kind!

Whatever lesson you want him to learn he has certainly thought of for hours! *Pained to behold.* Look – Edgar is my partner but Isabella has no one at all! You have Frances with whom to dance! Let Heathcliff come down and join us for just a short hour! The tyrant turns and walks away without a word. *Was in purgatory.* I climb up to the top of the stairs. The band from Gimmerton – fifteen strong – trumpet, trombone, clarionet, bassoon – french horns and base viol. I hold my hands over my ears and feel my wounds. *Had been locked up.* Cathy come down! Cathy come down! You are always so light on your feet! You are the lightest lass at the dance for miles around! *Entreaties were in vain.* Songs and carols – jigs and reels. I sit on the stairs and think of Heathcliff and blot out the sound.

"It's a cuckoo's sir – I know all about it: except where he was born and who where his parents, and how he got his money at first."

The swords flash in the sunshine.
The blood collects in pools.
The pirates fight most fiercely.
They swarm upon the deck.

A candle in the window of a distant room.
A peasant girl taking a sip of champagne.
A man who meets a spectre in the night.

A boy cries out in terror.
He is seized by brutal hands.
Stuffed within a sea-chest.
Keep ye there and make no sound.

Is there life beyond the earthly?
Water interfused with wine?
Do authors get to talk with their characters after they die?

The blood-soaked ship is silent.
Rigging creaks upon the deck.
The boy is crouched in terror.
Dare not breathe nor make a sound.

Ensconced with Heathcliff in the garret. I simply skittered along the roof. So I have torn a hole in my dress – so what of that?
A faery princess with a tear in her gown.
Come out, Heathcliff – come out. You can slip out and down to the kitchen. I shall have Ellen present you a meal. You have not eaten since yesterday's dinner – I am sure you have not. *Might be liberated.* Oh, don't be so sulky.

The world has not ended. When you are banished, my Heathcliff, then I am banished too. *Songs were going to cease.* I feel every welt on your person. I breathe every breath you breathe. Never in the history of human beings has anyone ever loved as have you and I. Whatever fortune makes of us, whether paupers or a king and a queen, we shall share what we have lost or we have gained. *How long I wait.* There is something in the air, Heathcliff – something is afoot. I know not what the future holds. Let us hope it will be to our gain. *I don't feel pain.* You are glum, but this too shall pass. Whatever good shall come to me shall come to you.

Chapter 5

Heathcliff 2

Keeper lying on the floor. Me lying beside him and reading a book. Everything clean and the fire damped down. Not much of a wind tonight. The clock ticks loudly when all is quiet. Waiting for nine o'clock to sound. Father is punctual as usual. He climbs the stairs and winds the clock. The Brontë Three break out the paper and the pens and the ink and get down to work.

A young boy brushing a pony in a barn.

She is bringing home the Lintons. They are to have a dance tonight. She will parade me out and present me to her friends. *Black and cross.* They will think that I am dirty. Hindley will force me to make a bow with the other servants. Then they will send me out to the barn to muck out the stalls. *Funny and grim.* She has asked me to wash my face. She has asked me to brush my hair. The Lintons don't want to meet me – she has told me so herself. Then why does she insist that I greet them when they come here? *You looked odd.* So I am that naughty swearing boy, am I? – the gypsy who took a rock to their precious dog? If they laugh at me I will blister their tender ears. *You are so dirty.* I had rather stay here in the stable. The new pony has a glossy coat. There's mucking manure and feeding do be done.

To be

A prince with manure on his hands.
A girl who is leading a false life.
A girl and boy splashing in a beck.

a crocus

How vast is the world of thought and wonder?
How minuscule is the world outside the mind?
Do you only come outside for bread and cheese?

growing out of melting snow.

Apples being pealed to make a pudding.
A causeway leading to a court.
A large old crumbling ancestral hall.

Spending the morning out on the moors. All alone and happy that way. If Cathy was here she would only be a pest.
A young boy admiring himself in a mirror.
Into the kitchen when I see they are gone – down the lane and off to church. Ellen has something for me on the table. Tea and cake and cheese. She has worked for weeks on the house for Christmas time. *Rich scent.* All right, if that's what you want. Make me decent – I'm going to be good. Make me into someone else if you think you can. *Shining kitchen utensils.* Brushing my hair – washing my face – dressing me smart. *Polished clock.* So Cathy grieved – so did I – her tears will dry. *Decked in holly.* Go up to her and apologize. Give her greeting at the door. *Silver mugs.* Ellen's advice and Ellen's fantasies. Emperor of China – Indian queen – high notion of my birth – a prince in disguise. *Scoured and well-swept floor.* Looking deeply into the glass – putting my arm out to the mirror as if to shake hands.

Always leaving on a path of springtime flowers. Soon returning on a path of dust and dung. It would seem that our lives fall into patterns. Sunlit meadows always pleased to open to him. Drizzling rain always poured down on his head.

"He'll love and hate equally under cover and esteem it a species of impertinence to be loved or hated again."

Hareton has gone to fetch some firewood! He is chopping the winter's wood! I seize the axe that he has been using! I kick the kindling away from my feet! I raise the axe up over my shoulder and strike the stump! I take an object from my pocket! I carry it around with me! It is the world – the globe – the earth! The place where people live! Everyone is an inhabitant except Cathy and me! I place it on the stump and swing the axe as hard as I can! Such a blow as splits the world in two!

All the flowers are praying - ink and paper - my soul-mate, keeper - milady drops a glove - broken pane of glass - it is early days - born out in the world - welcome to every soul - we can re-unite - wading and laughing.

We hardly spoke when we were children! We used very few words! We had no need for words to know that we agreed!

There was the agony of other people! Other people were only tolerable because of you! You were the only thing about earth that had beauty for me!

I longed to mingle my breath with yours! I yearned to fuse my blood with yours! For you and I to dissolve into mist upon the moors!

A street rat in Liverpool
assumed the crown would fit him too.

I take my stand in the kitchen. I straighten Ellen's cravat. I clench my teeth and then I open the door.
A young boy knocked to the floor with a vicious blow.
They are standing in a circle. Smothered in cloaks and furs. Her grand dress makes Cathy glow. *A rumbling sound.* But now I know she is not a stranger. I know I'm as good as any of them. I don't have to feel down-hearted. People breed sorrows for themselves. *Behold the two Lintons.* I am taller than Edgar Linton. Broader across the shoulders than he. I could knock him down in a twinkling. Edgar Linton looks like a little girl's doll beside me. *Taking a hand of each.* He sits home all day for a shower of rain. He trembles if he chances to meet a country lad. Dressed and rich and well-behaved perhaps, but Nelly says I can learn. I can dress and behave as well as ten-times he. *Brought them into the house.* I am about to hold out my hand, but Hindley puts his hand on my chest. Get this fellow out of the room! He pushes me through the door and comes in after me! He knocks me to the floor with a vicious blow!

The brilliant brother was losing his glow. Who would support these three sisters when their father's aid was withdrawn? Would they be paupers – would they be beggars? What was their value to the world? What would their means of livelihood turn out to be?

Making myself decent.
Greeting our guests at the door.

I am at the forge in Gimmerton! I brought my horse for a troubled shoe! The blacksmith has just stepped out for a moment! I seize the handle of the bellows and start to pump! I blow the fire to a raging blaze! The flames leap out towards my face! I need the fire at its hottest as there is something I want to do! I take an object from my pocket! I carry it around with me! It is the world – the globe – the earth! The place where people live! Everyone is an inhabitant except Cathy and me! I throw it in the hottest part of the flames! I seize the handle and fiercely pump the bellows again!

Beg for mercy - thrown yourself into a bog - atmospheric tumult - keep the fellow out - world outside the mind - think my quiet thoughts - finally give way - the unknown catherine - the writer of us all - things were simpler.

You took my hand in yours. You took Edgar's hand as well. You pressed our hands together, held by yours.

"You are a window on my wife's past. She hopes you'll feel welcome here. You'll be a reminder, along with Ellen, of what used to be."

Three cups were on the table and Nelly poured. Edgar took a napkin and wiped his hand. We three sat in your drawing-room with cups of tea.

"For music and dancing,
why the fiddle is for my son."

Hindley calling out to Joseph! Keep the fellow out of the room! Me lying on my back with blood on my lip!

A young boy burning his hand on the hob.

Hindley ordering me to the garret! Saying I'll cram my fingers in the tarts and steal the fruit! *Shoved him back.* Ellen speaks for me and almost gets a slap! *Sudden thrust.* If I were of size I would tear out Hindley's throat! *He'll touch nothing.* He kicks me as I am getting up! I fall back against the hob! I burn my hand quite fiercely but I will not let him know! *Make his head ache.* That hated Linton at the doorway! Spitting insults at me as he hides behind the door! I reach back towards the hob! I grab the handle of the tureen! I let it fling at my tormentor as he peeps through the door! Hot apple sauce all over his face and neck! *Snatched up the culprit.* The beating is worth the prize! I have bested Edgar Linton in front of Cathy! Edgar is crying like a child! Now how can she admire such a simpering knight at arms! I don't feel a thing as Hindley flails his arm!

A portrait with a subject effaced.
Servants siccing the dogs on intruders.
The consequences of being buried alive.

There is graveyard on two sides of the house. Burials too inside the church – under the floor. There are a number of Brontës have died. Our mother and our two sisters – Maria and Elizabeth. Gone but not forgotten – close to home.

Why so often walk on the moorlands?
Sun or rain – bog or trail?
What is the wind to you and what are you to the wind?

So the five of us are living in the house. It has its ups and downs. Father is Father – and getting older. Branwell is noticed when he is absent and noticed when he is at home. Charlotte and Anne each have a role. I do the baking and some other things. Between us all, we manage to get along.

The brilliant brother was losing his glow. Who would support these three sisters when their father's aid was withdrawn? Would they be paupers – would they be beggars? What was their value to the world? What would their means of livelihood turn out to be?

Darkness and glory \ a hush of peace \ nature's million mysteries \ time has altered me \ shake off the fetters \ the eye begins to see \ vanished like a vision \ a desolate desert \ warring day and night \ restored my earth.

A branch of a fir-tree touching a lattice.
A newspaper story about Sir Robert Peel.
A floor of smooth white stone.

Exposed in stormy weather / had no command of tongue / not my ghostly catherine / could discover them nowhere / have you forgotten me / unless some happy chance / i've dreamt, in my life, dreams / seasons of gloom and silence / one sensible soul / a glimpse of the abyss.

Lying here in the garret. Blood on my lip but I hardly feel a thing. I have other means to occupy my mind.
Eyes that cannot see a face.
Sounds of the dinner down below. Hearty laughter from Hindley, the host. Squeals of merriment from his wife. *Bountiful platefuls.* No doubt the Lintons are laughing too. If only I could see my Cathy's face. *Merry with lively talk.* Are her days of rebellion over? We used to sneer at politeness and gentility. We used to be castigated both. We would both turn up our noses in former times. *Mess of victuals.* What does she say when they simper and snivel? Is she not laughing at them with scorn? Why is Cathy not up here in the garret with me?

She kept the house, though she wasn't a servant.

I have risen from this table.
I have walked clean through this door.
I have walked right through this stile
and onto this moor.

"Yon lad gets war und war! He's left th' yate ut t' full swing, and Miss's pony has trodden dahn two rigs uh corn, un plottered through, raight o'er intu t' meadow!"

I am moving across the moors! Slow and steady is the word! I guide my horse where there is no trail! A landscape of furze and whinstone! A place where no one ever comes! There are mining pits and standing pools – a god-forsaken place! I must leave enough light so I can return before dark! I am come this far as there's something I yearn to do! I take an object from my pocket! I carry it around with me! It is the world – the globe – the earth! The place where people live! Everyone is an inhabitant except Cathy and me! I throw it as far as I can inside the bog.

Worlds of light - hereafter be denied admission - a mere husk - she has few hopes - second part of the plan - the three of us - look forward to the day - drowned in its waters - bothered to cut the leaves - seems rather ghost-like.

Hindley was sitting at the table. His reprobate friends were scattered around. He didn't get up and I didn't offer to shake his hand.

"I can't believe that you look so prosperous. All is forgiven, wouldn't you say? If you have money, you must join us at our cards."

I sat down and took out my purse. Hindley smiled as he saw my largess. I reached over and took the bottle and filled his glass.

She laughed and splashed and giggled.
"Let us let the water take us where it will."

Sounds of the dance from down below. The instruments of the Gimmerton band. Has even one of them wondered why Heathcliff is not there now?
Laughing people dancing to a band.
My ribs are used to a constant ache. It is my mind that throbs with passion. I have learned to take the pain and turn it to hate. *He might be liberated.* Revenge – revenge – revenge. Revenge with a gun – revenge with a knife – revenge with a rope or with a chain. *The excitement of the exercise.* Sounds of laughter and thumping feet. Christmas carols and songs and glees. Make you merry – make you merry, everyone. *The respectable houses.* What is the colour of Hindley's blood? What would Joseph say if I were to cut out his tongue? *A first-rate treat.* Let the whole world be merry while I think my quiet thoughts. The world is an hour-glass. I shall take their world and turn it upside down.

One night the old master dies in his sleep.

Being thrust into the garret.
Left to starve and plot my revenge.

He is not handsome! He is a Papist ! He is married! He is stern and he is abrupt! Very little has passed between us! We concentrate – we two – on the task at hand! A word or two of instruction and correction! Noble thought is the silent companion of the private man! He has the mind of a man of the superior type! He is improving my writing abilities! Every word that he utters is so in earnest! Every lesson is considered and concise! His sleeve, his cravat, his countenance! His conviction as he speaks! Every word carefully considered – precisely placed! We spend so little time together! I learn a page of French a day! He is impressed, I am sure, with my memory! His eyes issue praise though his lips do not! My special moment in each very busy day! And I am sure that he does not love his wife!

Talking nonsense by the hour - the blood that I lost - a man of great attraction - the mirror to your soul - tear him limb from limb - stomping on your grave - forces that constantly threaten - convinced i'm wrong - a quiet smile and a raging mind - face the globe.

Other people have your eyes! The Earnshaws have your eyes! The Lintons have them too!

Your daughter has your eyes! I find it hard to look at her! I have to wince and turn away!

Your daughter asked me once to speak of you! How could I tell her of you and me? It would be speaking to a person from another world!

Every day the lapwing would circle over her nest.
When the fledglings were all skeletons she flew away.

Cathy whispering through the boards. I do not answer. Cathy climbing in at the window. Tearing her fancy dress on a nail. I say not a thing.
A boy and a girl whispering in the dark.
Cathy speaking to me in the garret. Come down to the kitchen, Heathcliff. I have ordered Ellen to give you something to eat. *The prisoner.* The sounds of the singing. The sounds of the horns. The ugly squeaking of the violin. Everyone in the whole parish making merry but me. *Broken his fast.* Sit by the fire – get yourself warm – try to think of cheer-fuller things. *A quantity of good things.* Why does she want me to come down? So she can hustle back to the dance? So she can dance the night away with her conscience clear? *Sick and could eat little.* I let her drag me by the elbow. Out through the window and along the roof. Some day this roof will fall on Hindley's head.

"We crowded round, and over Miss Cathy's head I had a peep at a dirty ragged black-haired child, big enough to walk and talk."

The bonniest lass in the kingdom.
Lightest foot in the neighbourhood.
Every lad would like to dance with her.
Her hair with ringlets curled.

Two children running free across the moors.
Thorns reaching out for a hint of sun.
A handsome colt which goes lame.

Her laugh that was so cheerful.
Her smile that was so bright.
The music does not play for her.
The shadow of a frown.

Do you sense a throbbing membrane?
Sense the weight behind the dam?
Expect the hole in the dike to finally give way?

How now my bonny, bonny girl?
What makes ye ill at ease?
Does life so bright so soon go dark?
What choice is to be made?

I am alone without my Cathy. She thinks that what I am lacking is food. She has sent me into the kitchen and gone back to the dance.
A boy who is starving amidst a Christmas feast.
Ellen plies me on Cathy's behalf with cakes and pies. Elbows on knees – chin on hands – thinking my thoughts. Telling Nellie as I formulate my plans. My only fear is that Hindley will die before I extract my share of pain. I want to see him writhe and squirm like a crushed worm. *Our devil's psalmody.* Ellen is shocked and remonstrates loudly. For shame Heathcliff! Don't talk that way! It is for God to punish the wicked! We should learn to forgive! *Have the satisfaction.* I push her sweet-cake across the table. I want nothing but Hindley's blood. *Don't feel pain.* Very foolish to talk so to Ellen. Perhaps I have made a great mistake. From now on my vengeance will be silent. Simmer unnoticed on the hob. *Your gruel cold.* I will keep my notions quiet and bide my time.

Chapter 6

Cathy 3

There are days that never seem to end. There are days that seem to be nothing but questions. What of Tabby? – what of Father? – what of Branwell? What of Charlotte? – what of Emily? – what of Anne? What of Edgar? – what of Heathcliff? – what of Cathy? Ink is the balm that one applies to sooth the wounds.

A pauper sitting on a velvet throne.

Creeping into the kitchen. Trying not to make a sound. Asking Nelly if she is alone. *Are you alone.* Rocking Hareton on her knee. Singing soothing songs of childhood. Are you hoping he'll never grow up? *Disturbed and anxious.* Asking Nelly if Heathcliff is here. Oh why would it matter if he were here? He will know of it soon enough. It is good news if he will only see it that way. *I shan't help her.* Nelly begins to sing again. Telling Nelly that I am unhappy. She continues her trivial song. *Cant' make yourself content.* It is a boon for both of us! We would be peasants – Heathcliff – peasants! A begging bowl from door to door! Asking if Nelly can keep a secret. A secret from whom? *All the right in the world.* Hindley would never give us a cent if I married you! Nary a penny to buy our champagne! He would turn the both of us out in the pouring rain!

To be

A sea-storm subsiding magically.
A stranger among a brood of tigers.
A guest in a house who brings disease.

the saviour

Is Cathy you and are you Cathy?
Dreaming her dreams and thinking her thoughts?
Sharing the sunshine and the lightning in her skull?

of a family in peril.

A poem with changes for some of the words.
A fire of coal, peat and wood.
Children answering questions from behind a mask.

Telling her Edgar has asked me to marry. To marry, Nelly – marry! You are surprised, perhaps, with what goes on around here.
Two story-tellers wrangling over a tale.
Yes, I have given him an answer. No it won't be a secret from you. But first you must tell me your thoughts. Consent to marry or denial? – which would you have made in my place? Tell me truly what you think it ought to have been. *What I should do.* Why do you hesitate? – what is the matter? – why are you looking around the room? This is no silly matter of lullabies, Nelly. This is a question of a serious kind. *Whether I was wrong.* Well all right then, since you are so silent, I shall tell you what I have done. Edgar Linton has proposed to me and I told him in return, that I would be proud – I, Catherine Earnshaw – to be his wife. *Must say why.* So – what is the matter, Nelly? Why do you look so very odd? What objections could there possibly be in this world?

The younger sister was taken on as a governess. The boy of the household was in need of some Latin and Greek. Her brilliant brother was taken on to teach the boy. Then something went terribly wrong. The brilliant brother was dismissed from his post.

"I found him very intelligent on the topics we touched."

The walls of the world are breaking! There are cracks at all the seams! The vital fluid is slowly leaking from its core! I place my hands upon the surface! I press my palms against the globe! I try so hard to resist the leakage but I only have two hands and leaks are springing all over the surface of the globe!

Telling ancient tales - the concentrated essence - jerked back down to earth - peeping in at windows - find out what it is - they were invisible - wait in vain - bread and cheese - turn it upside down - ill at ease.

The loss of the blood that you see on the sill was not harmful to me! It simply means that I am becoming corporeal! I'm sure that it means that we can soon meet!

Meet me on the moors, my darling! Oh meet me at the kirk! Come after the daylight world has gone to sleep!

We must talk! Oh how we must talk! We must talk of all that has happened these twenty years!

The kingdoms' borders were rather murky.
There had been wars and treaties and things.

Nelly gives me the catechism. Testing the patience of a saint.
A servant explaining that life is not a fairy tale.
Have I made due consideration? – know what it means to pledge my word? – do I love Mr. Edgar? – why do I love Mr. Edgar? Oh why! why! why! why! why! Oh to be grilled in this way by a servant! *Ground under his feet.* Bad, bad, bad, is her only comment – bad to handsome! – bad to pleasant! – bad to young and bad to cheerful! *Air over his head.* And indifferent because Mr. Edgar should choose to love me! *Everything he touches.* Then she switches to worse and worse – worse that Edgar shall be rich! – worse that I shall be a great woman! The greatest woman, Nelly, in all the neighbourhood! *Every word he says.* And how? how? how? – as if it could matter! How do I love him, she wants to know. I give her a splendid answer, though I should not deign at all. The ground! – the air! – the everything! His looks! – his actions! – his words! *All his looks.* Why, why, why?, is her latest tactic. Why should I have to answer to why? So your questions are perfectly rational, Nelly, and my answers are perfectly not? This is what comes of raising one's servants above their place! *All his actions.* Oh this is so exasperating! Edgar is here and Edgar has asked me! – though there be princes and kings in the world! Would you want me to marry a poverty-stricken boy? *Entirely and all together.* I turn my face to the fire and collect my thoughts and control my beating mind. I shall live at Thrushcross Grange, Nelly, as the lady of the house! – and I shall have better servants than you have turned out to be!

The elder sister pondered the family dilemma at length. She decided that the sisters would open a school for girls. They set about to prepare themselves to that end. Two of the sisters travelled abroad to study languages. Before too long the younger sister left for home.

Telling Nelly my secret.
Telling Nelly I know I am wrong.

I hold my breath and look around me! There are people everywhere but they are paying no attention to the globe! They are sewing, reaping, eating but they do not look around! I must take each one by the elbow and explain! The globe is leaking vital fluid! This cannot be allowed to go on! I need everyone to stop their activities and turn away from their concerns and face the globe!

Reach out your arms and put your hands on the cracks in the fabric! Now push with all your might! I need everyone to help me! If you refuse then I no longer want to live!

Began to forthwith decipher - consider what next to write - hidden under a cloak - centre of both worlds - exactly what i think - she felt condemned - away from prying eyes - a terrified child - we must decide - a life with no substance.

My life was just too much for me! It was like burning at the stake! It was like gathering coals to stoke my funeral pyre!

I was scorched while in your presence! While with Edgar I was turning to ice! I never melted nor ever froze when I was a child!

You were the highwayman at the crossroads! Edgar the tally-man in the fields! You both had studied at the Hindley-the-tyrant school!

The princess aspired to climb to the top of the tower.
It was cloud-capped so she stood on the back of a frog.

Oh but Nelly – listen Nelly! I am so sure that I am wrong!
A dreamer who is stinting of her dreams.
I have dreams – Nelly – dreams! I dream dreams that stay with me! That play havoc with my ideas! Dreams that turn my every feeling and thought quite upside-down! *To be my home.* My mind is as water – Nelly – water – but a dream can be like wine, and colour every thought that one has come to count upon. No I don't mean ghosts and visions – I mean dreams with the stamp of the real. *Come back to earth.* I tell Nelly my dream about heaven – how the angels were quick to anger – how they flung me out on the heath. I never saw angels who were angrier than were these. *Angels were so angry.* The other dream I cannot tell you! No – cannot and never will! The dream of heaven of which I told you will have to do!

A girl reaching her hand through broken glass.
A bitter whirlwind of suffocating snow.
A young shepherd who is afraid to go home.

Bitter cold at times. Snow in the wintertime. Fog, sleet, hail – all of those. Winter is summer waiting for spring – all the hills purple with heather as I walk along.

Are you as dark in thought as Heathcliff?
Are yours the hands that do his deeds?
Are you the creature who provides the demonic spark?

What's this about writing novels? Charlotte and Anne and I? Who would make up such a story about us three? Sure we sit at the dining-room table. Every night, after nine o'clock. After the household settles down. When Father is in his bed. When Branwell is out on the town. Charlotte on one side and Anne on the other. We are thinking of starting a school. French and German are what young ladies are expected to learn. You'll hear nothing of writing novels while talking with me.

The elder sister pondered the family dilemma at length. She decided that the sisters would open a school for girls. They set about to prepare themselves to that end. Two of the sisters travelled abroad to study languages. The younger sister was taken on as a governess.

Bursting the fetters \ the struggle of distress \ the fearful and the fair \ the vital sap \ break the chain \ pulse begins to throb \ deserts frozen dry \ shadows on shadows \ could not hold them all \ all through the night.

A pair of colts purchased at the parish fair.
A two-story limestone parsonage.
A garden-gate at the end of four-miles walk.

Craving alms of the sun / the corner of his eyes / as if it came from the devil / have a ramble at liberty / like devil's spies / as if I were a goblin / I'm convinced I'm wrong / reflected a score of glittering moons / faint dawn of progress / I'm sure I should be myself.

Do you understand me, Nelly? Let me tell you clearly then.
A girl bidding farewell to a child.
I have no more business to marry Edgar than to dwell in heaven. But who am I to marry? *Flung me out.* Hindley has put me in this spot. Wuthering Heights is teetering on the cliff-side. It will someday have a great fall. *Sobbing for joy.* It is either a roof or a rainstorm. Heathcliff will be bereft as well. We cannot be children forever, Heathcliff and I.

Nothing eventful ever happened to her.

Mild the day and mild the journey.
Cruel the day and cruel the path.
I have been all at Thrushcross Grange.
I have been all at Wuthering Heights.

"Hahsomdiver, t'maister 'ull play t' devil to-morn, and he'll do weel. He's patience itsseln wi' sich careless, offald craters – patience itsseln he is!"

Only two are left to help me! They are on opposite sides of the globe!

Put your hands on the side of the world and press them in! I ask each one in turn, but they both refuse! But everyone else is helping! Why will you two not comply? Can you not see what I am seeing? The vital fluid is leaking steadily from the globe! I have said – you heard me say it – that if even one of the many millions refuses to plug the hole in the globe and retain the vital fluid, I would rather die! My life is in your hands! You heard me say! – you heard me say! – and yet you refuse?

A story to enact - this extraordinary man - out of her head - a cover for your eyes - feeding him to his dogs - never had any conception - only one force - accidently overhearing a tale - fling it out of doors - a ship trapped in the ice.

Oh, do you remember that day when Edgar – and Isabella – came to call? And you were lingering in the kitchen? And I kept trying to get you to go out into the fields?

Oh, I was betraying you – and I knew it – and I felt so terribly low! But something was pulling me – quite forcefully – the other way! I was bartering your heart for a sugar-plum!

But I don't know whether forgiveness is at issue! I see no point in forgiving the past! How did we get so mired in this bog? – how do we get out?

The Devil was visiting Heaven.
Negotiations were taking place.
St. Peter was busy so the Devil answered the door.
The girl who had knocked quickly turned and walked away.

I tell you Nelly, I don't live in dreams. I live in the present – of money and food.

A teller of tales who chooses carefully whom to tell.

Facing reality is your specialty. Here is something the both of us know. It would degrade me, Nelly, to marry Heathcliff now. *Explain my secret.* Nelly starts and looks past my shoulder. She almost forgets the babe in her arms. *Heathcliff so low.* Why what is the matter, Nelly? Come Nelly – why do you start? Is that Joseph – come in at the door? Surely it can't be Heathcliff? In this early from the fields? *It would degrade me.* Well, it is no matter now. I have said nothing I won't tell him someday. Surely Heathcliff couldn't hear me at the door.

The young master banishes the young boy to the stable.

Battered by tumult and by torrent.
Yearning for Heathcliff to come again.

Lying awake for a moment or two before I sink, thankfully, into sleep –

at the end of a long and exhausting day. Oh, I cannot believe the amount of turmoil and toil. Exhausting – completely exhausting – those children have shaken me like a rag. To speak that way to an adult – to insult and belittle and tease – I have never known children to speak and to act in such a manner as this. That I must control the little angels but never discipline them at all – why cannot the parents see this as an impossible task? And if I report calumny, cruelty, malignancy – as traits to be nipped, at once, in the bud – why the parents look down at me coldly and blame it on me. The parents' blindness is causing their children a world of harm. To know the ideal – as clearly as the sun is seen to shine through a stained-glass window – and yet to have no power to be the cause of its realization – that is the worst of the burden which I have been charged to bear. These children will suffer when they are adults – I see misery in their lives when they go out in the world. I only hope that I can sleep – I shall be direly in need of the sustenance come the morrow. I have planted the seeds of my counsel – they are waiting and eager to grow – it is the parents who are blocking out the sun.

The world without - free to change the words - passing me in turn - i am heathcliff - the flames of the dancing fire - what care me you - a servant is a servant - an unknown tongue - that silly book - no air to breathe.

Is it twenty years? – is it twenty? – can it actually be? This means that my child will soon be of age! My own child will soon be older than me!

Oh what a wonderful thought to have! That my child – my own little girl – will have a life much longer than mine! She will go through changes here on earth – will know what it is to be human and alive – for much longer than I was ever able to be!

Oh we should have talked with each other! We should have talked and talked and talked! I am so sorry that I chided you so on that final day!

Climbing the magic faery mountain.
Feeling exhausted from the climb.
Bits of gold-leaf breaking off and skittering down.

So what is this talk about desertion? Nelly, what nonsense you sometimes talk.

A tale in which the world is null and void.

Oh I could never forsake my Heathcliff. That is not what this is about. Edgar Linton must know the price that must be paid. *Shall never know.* I have praised Heathcliff enough in his presence – told him that diamonds are found in a roughish state and must be polished ere displayed. Surely Edgar would have no objections as you have raised. *More myself than I am.* So I tell her about the rock – how it is always under my feet – about the foliage that comes and goes with the winter and the spring. *Our souls are made of.* I would let all the Lintons perish, Nelly – I would push them myself off the cliff. If they were gone and the world was a void he would still remain. I would never give up Heathcliff to gain Thrushcross Grange. *An existence of yours beyond you.* Heathcliff will be second man of the neighbourhood – he will be Edgar's brother in law – he will ride a fine horse and tie a fine cravat. *The use of my creation.* He will dine off plate that is polished in silver and gold – learn to speak and act as the educated do – listen to music in drawing rooms and make fine chatter outside the church – become the prince that you wondered if he might be. *Entirely contained here.* I have always been Heathcliff, Nelly, and he has always been me. I have always known his trials and felt his pain. That time his ribs were broken – why then my ribs ached too. And every welt that Hindley has put on his back has been put on my back too. I feel every misery that he is subjected to. How many times I have cried that he has not been seen as exactly what he is. Not by my father, not by my mother, not by Hindley – and not even you. But I shall work on Edgar, Nelly, day by day and night by night. You shall see – you shall soon see. Those two will be as thick as are Heathcliff and I. *My great thought in living.* So what is all this about Heathcliff? What do you mean he might have heard? What do you mean he was here and went out? Surely Heathcliff couldn't have heard me from the door!

"Indeed its face looked older than Catherine's; yet when it was set on its feet, it only stared round and repeated over and over again some gibberish that nobody could understand."

A girl waits on her balcony.
Above her is the moon.
The clock it has been silenced.
It will not chime tonight.

A girl who wills herself to die.
A child left on a landing overnight.
Honeysuckle bushes embracing a thorn.

A knight rides through the gateway.
He rides from out a book.
He rides a noble charger.
Her favours on his lance.

Giving birth to all these characters?
Enjoying their smiles and enduring their pain?
Lying down with those who are silent in the grave?

He climbs upon the ivy vines.
Full armour on has he.

He lights upon the balcony.
She swoons into his arms.

The rain pours down in torrents. I sit here by the wall.
A girl who shares her soul with someone else.
Heathcliff has not come home tonight. He was not out in the fields. Nelly told me that he was right there in the kitchen all that time. That he left at the word 'degrade' and missed the rest. *Continue to be.* Wind and rain and thunder. No I don't want a shawl or a bonnet. I will stay if it takes the night. I want to speak to him as soon as I am able. What will I say to him when he returns? What will Heathclliff say to me? He is not a man of words, but a man of heart. *A mighty stranger.* Oh I must be able to talk to him. Tell him all that I have thought. We have never talked of our future. We have never shared our thoughts. What is he doing out in this rainstorm? Where shall he live if he has run off? *The eternal rocks beneath.* We shall never be parted, Heathcliff. You are always in my thoughts. Head to head, heart to heart, soul to soul. *I am Heathcliff.* Oh I hope I catch pneumonia. I hope I die before you come home. What a miserable wedding day. I would be happier in the churchyard than in the church. *My own being.* I do all of this for you. Let the rain come down in torrents. You must hear every word I have to say.

Chapter 7

Heathcliff 3

Eight o'clock of an evening – Father fires his gun. The house assembles – the family worships. Father locks and bars the door – tells us not to stay up late. Climbs the stairs – winds the clock – loads the pistol. The end of the day for him. We unbar the door for Branwell, set our writing paraphernalia out on the table and sit down and begin to write once again.

A house in which a family is at odds.

Coming in from the field to the kitchen. Wondering what is the cause of this row. Bawling and yawling fit to wake up the fiends of hell. *Wholesome terror.* Hindley and Ellen in an argument. They often fight like cats and dogs. *Mad beast's fondness.* She is worried about the soul of that young brat, Hareton. Perhaps if Hindley should go to church! – perhaps if Hindley wouldn't drink! – perhaps if Hindley would be the little boy he used to be! *Madman's rage.* Ellen is always talking of things that will never come true. It is a battle for Hindley's soul – Ellen – and I am winning as we stand. People say I am the reprobate – all the word in the neighbourhood – but Hindley is passing me in the turn. *Flung into the fire.* I never thought I would see him cry but the loss of that woman set him off. I smiled to myself to see him grovel in such pain. *Like a dog.* But Ellen – so foolish of you to think that Hindley cries for his flesh and his blood. Look at the way he treats his son and heir. He has cast the boy aside, Ellen – a cuckoo invading his nest. *By heaven and hell.* He hates the boy for the loss of his wife. Gambling and drink – drink and gambling. He is destroying what you choose to call his soul. He will soon destroy the boy if I have my way.

To be

A young girl, motionless and mute.
Eyes evincing scorn and desperation.
A nightmare that lasts for forty years.

estranged from the one

Suppose you'd been born in an earlier time?
Suppose you'd been born in another place?
An Irish colleen, perhaps, or a Cornish lass?

who shares one's soul.

Kneading dough while reading a book.
A few mildewed books piled up in a corner.
A wash-house, a privy and a well.

I stand here under the stairs. Enjoying the wrangling on the landing. Ellen and Hindley go on and on.
A boy who is planning out his life.
Screaming and squealing from the boy. His is terrified of his father. *The carving knife.* Ellen's blood is running quite coldly. Hindley is holding a knife in her mouth. He is fixing to slit her throat. *Rather be shot.* Ellen is talking to him quite calmly. Perhaps I could sneak into the kitchen and take in hand a butcher knife. What would the law decide to do if I send him to hell? Would I swing if I were to jerk him under the ribs? – would they say that the master was murdered by his slave? *Flaying alive.* Perhaps I should put in a word for Ellen – she has shown me compassion at times – I would rather he not slit her throat. Now if he were threatening his son and heir – I should let him carve.

Something about falling in love with a married lady. Something about acquiring her estate when her husband died. Something about a cruel passage in the husband's will. Something about a barrier between his love and he. Something about true love being thwarted by the gods.

"It is astonishing how sociable I feel myself compared with him."

I am standing out in the cold! I try to move but am held back! A clasp around my neck and a chain! I feel along the chain and detect a pole! I am chained to a pole in frigid air! It is dark and I am alone! My blood is turning to ice! Where is Cathy? Where has she gone? Why on earth am I chained here all alone?

A pack of dogs - the fool's craving to hear - we agree to exchange - every
window is a mirror - chills the marrow - two troubled houses - pressed against

the glass - crown would fit - the private man - so soon go dark.

We used to go running out on the moors! I never felt so free or so safe! We never saw another human being!

No one to scold us and no one to beat us! Occasionally a boy with a handful of sheep! There seemed to be only you and me for hundreds of miles!

We explored the moors together! A lapwing's nest – a faery cave! It was a whole wide world unpeopled – just you and me!

A prince and a princess happened to meet along the way.
"Excuse me," said one to the other, "but I find myself rather lost.

What to do with this wretched child? I stand and hold him in my arms. I could smash his head against the wall and no one would know.

A child in a cradle of outstretched arms.

What would the law do with Hindley – a man who has murdered his son and heir? *Unnatural cub.* Would they cast him into the dungeon? – stretch his neck with a velvet rope? *Such a monster.* Cathy's brother – but what of that? Cathy's nephew – but what of that? She has called Hindley a tyrant time and again. Would she choose Hindley over me if she should find out it was I who dispatched the child? *Break the brat's neck.* Ellen has seen me catch the child. She is reaching out her arms. If it were dark I would gladly have battered out the brains. *Squalling and kicking.* No – I will keep Hindley and Hareton alive. I want them both to suffer slowly – as do I.

The eldest sister was left alone in a foreign city. A pupil-teacher in a religious pensionat. French and German were the languages she studied. But she was lonely – very lonely. In her room at night she yearned to be back home.

Thwarting my own revenge.
Daydreaming on the bench.

The clouds begin to part! I can see the curve of the earth! Through the clouds I can see water! The Atlantic or the Pacific! So I am chained to one of the Arctic poles! At one of the ends of the earth! Where is Cathy? Where has she gone? The air is getting colder! My blood is a turgid stream! I tug at the chain that restrains my neck, but I cannot budge!

Blood upon the bark - the slavering jaws - swear a mutual curse - kill me with desire - say very little - a message for cathy - clinging to the ledge - we live very simply - a fork of a path - a circle without any magic.

So where was I for those three long years? Was I guiding maharajas, on the backs of lumbering elephants, in a hunt for lions in the jungles of exotic lands? Or was I lying in a puddle – stupefied with drink – on the cobblestones of an alley in Liverpool?

One thing is for certain, Cathy! Make no mistake about that! No matter where I was, all of my thoughts were fully occupied with you!

Wherever I was, I heard plenty of stories! The story of the dodo who tried so hard to be an eagle would make you laugh! The story of the eagle who tried so hard to be a dodo would make you cry!

"Are my slippers hurting your back?" the princess asked the frog.
The frog merely grunted in reply.

Sliding down on the back-kitchen bench. I shall do no work today. About Hindley and Hareton I have need of further plans.

A young man making plans for others' lives.

I have done myself a bad turn. I have rescued the son and heir and no doubt he will treat me worse than does Hindley, in time to come. *The critical moment.* I let it slip right through my fingers. The father kills the son and then the father goes to the gallows – then Cathy, the only heir, inherits the farm – and the lord of the manor, I, in the course of time. It was perfect and I let it slip away. *A natural impulse.* Hindley is sliding straight to hell, with my assistance. Ellen takes away his drink – I give it back to him and more. The long slow road to perdition, but much too slow. *Made himself the instrument.* There has to be more than just the drink. Kenneth says that Hindley will live to a good long age. Perhaps he will burn the whole place down around his ears – a thing he often threatens, himself, to do. No – there must be something I can do – not something he does himself. I want both Hindley and Hareton in my snare.

A stranger among a brood of tigers.
A hand-written story inside a printed book.
A man who fears being buried in snow.

The postman comes to the door. The Leeds Intelligencer. Blackwoods – a borrowed magazine. Talk of politics and poetry. Always plenty of new ideas.

Suppose you'd never heard of Haworth?
Never taken a walk on the moors?
Would either one rate a dot on your personal globe?

My dog is my constant companion. I like to lie with him on the floor. I read a book while he sleeps off his run. I take him out for exercise every day – whatever the weather – rain or shine. I whistle for him when he gets too far away. When I sit at the table, he lies beside my chair. He is always in very great need of attention. Oh yes you are, Keeper! – yes you are! If I take my hand off your head, you emit a loud groan! I lock him in the kitchen when I go to bed.

The elder sister pondered the family dilemma at length. She decided that the sisters would open a school for girls. They set about to prepare themselves to that end. Two of the sisters travelled abroad to study languages. The younger sister was taken on as a governess.

Breaking the bars \ mute music \ true to myself \ the narrow dungeon \ the waste of youth \ brain to think again \ the perished spring \ earth was lost \ all are held in me \ your glorious eyes.

A family sitting room without a lobby or passage.
A girl with her feet on the fire-grate.
A house exposed to stormy weather.

The corners defended / the air swarmed with catherines / maintaining til dusk a struggle / was altered considerably / to repair some of his wrongs / convinced I'm wrong / an existence of yours beyond you / I'm not a stranger / believed no such thing.

Cathy enters in a hurry. She calls for Ellen, not for me. What is so secret that she must ask if they are alone?
A young man accidently overhearing a tale.
Cathy is singing the praises of Edgar. How he walks and talks and simpers. Like praising her pet dog or her favourite horse. *Are you alone.* Something about Edgar being handsome and a pleasure to be with. *Disturbed and anxious.* Someday Hindley will be dead – or better yet, a helpless cripple. And Cathy and I will be the masters of this house. Hindley will sit there in his chair – a mute, a lame, a cripple. *Instead of a sentence.* Something about Edgar being youthful and cheerful. *I shan't help her.* He will not have the use of his tongue – he will not have the use of his arms. He will be starving at our feast. He will envy the dogs who lick the crumbs from the floor. A crust of bread and a sip of water once a day. *Keep a secret.* Something about Edgar being rich. Something about Cathy becoming the first lady of the neighbourhood. *Her own concerns.* Oh I could talk like those aristocrats if I chose. Did you enjoy yourself at the opera? Did you prance along the avenue in a coach and four? Have you seen the latest ball-gowns in the seamstress's shop?

She lived mostly inside her own mind.

Seen and been the girl in the tree.
Seen and been the boy on the grass.
Seen and been the old man on his journey.
Seen and been the young boy in his care.

"Bud he'll not be soa allus – yah's see, all on ye! Yah mun'n't drive him out of his heead for nowt!"

In the distance I can see Cathy! Her head is above the horizon! Her back is turned to me! So she is chained to the other Arctic pole! The cold must be painful for her too! But she is not alone! She is chatting with another person! I can see their frosty breath! She has a companion in her misery while I am alone! I try to shout, but I cannot speak! If only she knew that I am here! She doesn't turn! She doesn't see! She doesn't know! The darkness falls! The air grows colder! I tug at the chain!

Which kingdom would you say - converted into a stranger - my great thought in living - found the very core - he is a monster - nothing that nelly can say - locks and bars the door - inside her own mind - that gypsy brat - combined them in two volumes.

I was a ghost from the day I left! As you were a ghost at Thrushcross Grange! I couldn't tell you where I was for those three long years!

I was moving among the crowds but I used to wonder if they could see me! When I spoke I didn't recognize my voice! I would see them as if through water, though they could see me!

And where did I get my money? – my fancy clothes and my fine cravats? Hindley's friends asked where I had been, but I didn't know! The secret I kept from them was a secret from me!

St. Peter was visiting Hades.
Negotiations were taking place.
The Devil was busy so St. Peter answered the door.
The boy who had knocked quickly turned and walked away.

Cathy is speaking to Ellen of heaven. Give me time, Cathy – time. You shall see how the future will bless us. We shall have heaven here on earth. *Angry angels peeking over the side of a cloud.* Something about heaven not being her home. *So many friends.* We shall be masters of this kingdom. We shall own this whole estate. We shall dance on Hindley's grave. We shall put Hareton out in the fields from morning til night. *So few cares.* Something about angels getting angry. *Make yourself content.* Like the way I comb my hair? Like the way I click my heels? Like the way I wedge fragments of French between my verbs? *All the right in the world.* Something about being flung out of heaven onto the heath. *What I should do.* Like how I scribble with ink and paper? Like how I kiss you on the hand? Would you rather I should kiss you on the cheek? *Whether I was wrong.* Something about marrying Edgar Linton instead of me.

The young girl and the young boy run free on the moors.

Listening to Cathy talk of her dreams.
Walking to Liverpool in the pouring rain.

Lydia Gisborne! – Lydia Robinson! – Lydia Brontë! She is writing these names in a book! Over and over again! Searching for the essence of her soul! And the essential her – she no doubt realizes – is dependent upon her union with the essential me! She hastens at a noise! A capital idea! Hurry! Hurry! Hurry! Hiding her true thoughts among her other books on the shelf! Safe from prying eyes! The essential me will one day be her lord and master! The true successor to her husband's vast estate! Her former husband will be forgotten by us both! It will be as if he had he never existed at all! She herself has barely existed – she has had no life at all! Until she met me, her existence was dull and void! Her lips move silently as her hand lingers caressingly on the book! Sentiments that she will one day whisper in my ear! We shall meld into each other day by day!

Painted himself out - all of our differences - his chest against the flow - have a strange presentiment - my head is reeling - dark ink on a white page - what is this barrier - cannot read the signals - a path of springtime flowers - a child once more.

I never ever looked ahead! I would wake up and every day would look the same! I never thought that anything could ever change!

Until you deserted me, I had no thoughts of aggression! Nor accumulation! – nor acquisitiveness! I never wanted to own anything – stick of yew or clutch of heather – nothing at all!

But then I saw how the world was tending – you were my mentor, Cathy – you! I saw I had nothing that anyone wanted – nothing for which anyone envied me! You judged a sovereign of greater weight than a shared-soul!

Waiting in line to make a humble presentation.
Yawning and rubbing the eyes and giving the head a shake.
Bowing down and kissing the ring of the faery queen.

First lady of the neighbourhood! You shall have a coach and four! And we shall hold our noses up as we ride to church! All the peasants will line the path as we walk up the lane!

Three people standing at an altar.

Something about Hindley, her wicked brother. *Whether I should have.* And how has the weather been, Milord? Finding life to be a chore? Let us all pray to God for a little less rain. *Many things to be considered.* Something about Hindley bringing me low. *Can be answered properly.* Oh I admire your rows of servants. Each of them bowing in his turn. All of them scrambling when Milady drops a glove. *The following catechism.* Something about marrying Edgar Linton. Something about how it would degrade her to marry Heathcliff – how it would degrade her Ladyship's self to marry me. *Speak rationally.* Marry me, Lady Catherine – marry me! We could go from door to door begging alms! Seek shelter from the winter winds in our faery cave! Muck out the stables together in our velvet clothes!

"I was frightened, and Mrs. Earnshaw was ready to fling it out of doors; she did fly up, asking how he could fashion to bring that gipsy brat into the house."

The winter winds blow coldly.
The snow it blows with force.
It covers up the valleys.
It crests upon the hills.

Angry angels flinging a girl out on the heath.
Two waifs peering in at a window.
Gunpowder lying as harmless as sand.

A lonely figure wanders.
This man has lost his way.
There are pits beside the pathway.
There is danger in the bog.

What then would be Emily Brontë?
What then would be Heathcliff and Cathy?
What then would your great life's work have been?

He left a warming fireplace.
The people were so cold.
His face and hands are numbing.
He will die of their neglect.

Walking miles and miles and miles. Checking the signposts every so often for Liverpool. I never should have came here with the old man.
A young boy seeking shelter from a storm.
The rain pours down in torrents. Walking in puddles up to my knees. Hoping I fall in one and drown or get lost in a bog. *Got no answer.* Cathy how could you do this to me? How could you do this to yourself? Fine clothes – fine manners – fine house? Is this what has come between us? *Heard a good part.* No doubt you are warm and snug in your bedroom – dreaming dreams of what is to be – you in your wedding gown and the peasants lining the walk. *The*

gate is open. I shall break a board off this barn. If I don't I shall drown before I get my revenge. *Out of hearing.* You and Edgar gleaming and smug. The finest pair in the neighbourhood. Waving to the peasants as you leave in your coach and four. *Make him re-enter.* Oh your coachman is so handsome in his mistress's uniform! Such a pity that his hands are never clean!

Chapter 8

Cathy 4

Interesting thoughts today, in church. I find myself moving in and out of Father's sermons. He glances down at me at times. He knows I take in every word. We never talk of such at home. His thoughts are his and mine are mine. We both know it will always be this way. I never go when the curates preach. I hear them chatter here in the house and that's enough. The distillation of words and silence produces ink.

A table with three cups of tea.

The first lady of the neighbourhood. The days go on and on. Fond of Edgar – Fond of Isabella – fond, fond, fond. Fond of them as they are fond of me. If it's too cold we stay inside – if it's too hot we stay inside. We read our books and play our music and sing our songs. We go to church on Sunday mornings and chatter idly at the door. Never a Hindley nor a Hareton do we see. *Honeysuckles embracing the thorn.* Edgar is wonderfully patient – Isabella fears my tongue. They avoid my storms and enjoy my sunny days. A stroll in the park with an umbrella. Now and again, a carriage ride. Nelly is smug but is good for Edgar. She is in touch with his every mood. She is much better here, as am I, than at Wuthering Heights. *Gunpowder lay as harmless.* It is a life that seems rather ghost-like – like a life with no substance at all – a life for which my fingers have no feel. A game of cards, a cup of tea, an open window when the wind is calm. A circle without any magic – Isabella, Edgar and me. *Seasons of gloom and silence.* Perhaps they see me as absent-minded. Ellen certainly does, I know. I think of Heathcliff and what he might be doing at every minute of every day. He was so wrong to take himself out of my life in that way.

To be

Rambling about in the thick of a snow-storm.
The consequences of being buried alive.
The fingers of a little ice-cold hand.

called on to explain

Why your great love of animals?
Do you serve them or do they serve you?
Do you feel you lock them up or set them free?

what one has been.

Clouds moving slowly across the hills.
A billowy white ocean of fallen snow.
A table and chairs in a dining room.

A man from Gimmerton? A man from Gimmerton?
Three people clasping hands in a drawing-room.
No man from Gimmerton at all! It is Heathcliff! – wonderful Heathcliff! Returned to me as from the dead! *Coming from the garden.* I take his hands! – I tell him how wonderful! Where have you been? – what have you done? – why so long away without a word or two? Oh you have been so cruel to me as you cannot conceive. Edgar and I have been lonely here without our Heathcliff. It will all be different now. *Is it really you.* I get up and take his hands and gaze in his eyes. I scarcely know what he is saying. His eyes flash so as he talks. *Out of her head.* Edgar will love him as a brother. Love is a garden of infinite growth. Surely Edgar can see the love I bear for both. He will be welcome here as often as his own life will allow. *Make a jubilee.* Perhaps a wife – perhaps some children – a Heathcliff circle of his own. That he will be dwelling at the Heights will mean that he is close. *Breathless and wild.* I rise up and take his hands again. I thrust Edgar's hand in his. He in turn takes Edgar's hand. I hold both hands in mine. I gaze from face to face. *A marvelous treasure.* Heavenly happiness here on earth. Love for me is love for all. I am the one who brings us together. I draw a perfect circle round us all.

He returned home to live with his father and his sisters. No longer the most brilliant boy in the parish. No longer to be the brilliant writer of promise. No longer the brilliant painter of the Queen and her court. His brass was tarnished – he seemed to have no future at all.

"The tone in which these words were said revealed a genuine bad nature. I no longer felt inclined to call Heathcliff a capital fellow."

It is an angel with extraordinary wings! What do you want with me, I ask!

Why do you beckon instead of speak? Don't you know that I cannot stay here? I have a bundle in my arms! Something precious that I cannot forsake! You must let me go back down and be on my way! You are a stranger to the earth! There are things that happen there that you cannot know!

Attacking an intruder - oh wicked, wicked - my only offering - cannot go on from here - write of the day's events - a voice crying out - all I shall ever have - good as any of them - every word carefully considered - leave the latch unlatched.

So you have felt my presence, have you? Well rest assured that I have felt the presence of you! Your breath upon my cheek has been as real to me as you say my breath on your cheek has been real to you!

I have been unable to break through this barrier! I can feel it with my hands! The first time I managed to reach beyond was when I took the frightened gentleman by the hand!

I have often come here, of late, to the window! I expected a better welcome than was offered by that fine gentleman! Though the blood that he drew did no damage that I am able to perceive!

"I have a story to enact when I get where I need to be.
Which kingdom would you say we are in right now?"

I am elated! Oh I am elated! I pull at Nelly's hair! Oh how can you sleep at this juncture? It is a whole new existence for me!

A woman waking a servant late at night.

Heathcliff has returned to Wuthering Heights! And he will be welcome at the Grange, Nelly, no matter what Edgar might say. Edgar is just a little slow to see what must be. *Too great to be real.* Oh, don't be so quick to feel superior, Nelly. You think you see problems that your mistress cannot possibly see. Heathcliff and I have a bond, Nelly – we correspond without speech. He and I have a secret language – it has silence at its core. But I grant you that with Edgar everything between us must be said. *A half-civilized ferocity.* Oh, I admit I made a mistake, Nelly – I did a foolish thing – I decided to suffer in silence while Heathccliff was away. A major mistake on my part. I should have praised Heathcliff's merits. I should have prepared Edgar for this day. Oh but Heathcliff is so contrary – how would I know that he would come storming through our door? *Gaze fixed on him.* There were times I never expected to see him alive again, you know, Nelly. I would hear strange noises – I would think strange thoughts – I would flinch and wonder if Heathcliff had suffered a knock. I was everywhere Heathcliff was, Nelly – I could sense but I couldn't see. Was I strolling through a bazar, do you think? – was I a captive who chaffed in my chains? Elation and despair – gentle breezes and sweltering skies. *Feared he would vanish.* There was a membrane through which I could feel but couldn't perceive. I was living another life as I strolled in the garden and gazed out the window and sat in church and read a book and sat with Edgar and Isabella and sipped my tea. Every joy that Heathcliff knew brought a hint of red to my cheeks. Every agony Heathcliff suffered I suffered too. *Absorbed in their mutual joy.* Yes with Edgar, all is different. I must be told if Edgar has broken a fingernail. Even so, I will bring Edgar along quite quickly, Nelly, as you shall certainly see. He will see Heathcliff as his twin when I get through. And the same will be true of Heathcliff. Both Heathcliff and Edgar love me and that is my key.

The headmaster was a man of great attraction. He was erudite, remote and brilliant. He was demanding but quite compassionate. He was scholarly and he was wise. Everything she had always imagined in a man. She fell deeply in love with this extraordinary man.

Overwhelmed by the sight of a ghost.
Welcoming Heathcliff into the family at the Grange.

Another angel appears! This one beckons and gestures too! No, I will not stay here! I have reason why I must go! Each one takes me by an arm! Their fingers bite into my flesh! I almost drop my bundle! I twist my shoulders and wrench my arms! I tear myself free and run a few steps! I see arms out down below! Hands are reaching towards the clouds! I take another couple of steps! I toss my bundle down to whomever is down below!

He who suffered here - about the difficulties - why so painful - a box of soldiers - nothing I wish to share - gone to hell or heaven - unlined and blank - something you've written about - the only test - the thick of a snow-storm.

I used to sit Edgar down in his chair. Yes, I sat upon his lap. Just to ask him what is important? – what are our needs?

What the tea and what the sugar? What the meat and what the broth? But we didn't have a language that we both could talk.

I took the sugar-bowl and poured it out on the table. What we need and what we don't need. Would you go all the way to China – Edgar – for a cup of this watery tea?

"The tower is very high," the princess sighed to the frog.
"Would you mind standing up on tippy-toes?"

So where did Heathcliff go I wonder? What did Heathcliff do? Where has he been gone these three long years?
A person pouring poison on another's dream.
Did he find his own true self? A sewer-rat or the son of a king? Oh I love

him though I don't know him – he is the other half of me. People wonder about the other side of the moon. *Show a great weakness.* Is he a prince of all the Indias? Is he from China – or from Japan? Sometimes I think he takes in all of the world. Angels and devils have often gone out in the world in disguise. What did our mother think and not say? What did our father know and not tell? *Spoiled children.* All I know is that I am Heathcliff and he is me. We have always made one together. Why is Edgar so slow to share my thoughts with me? *Consequence to both sides.* Nelly is quick to sound a warning. Oh I don't regret what has happened. It will all work out in the end. *Fight to the death.* But we would be much better off without Nelly. She is the one who puts things in my head. I never ever doubted Heathcliff without a Nelly conversation in my head. I never ever doubted Edgar without the same. She is the one who poisons every dream I dream.

Eyes evincing scorn and desperation.
A dream which a person never tells.
A path with a bog on either side.

Prayers in the morning – prayers at night. The bells of Haworth church. Children streaming to Sunday School. Long hours on the black oak pew. Cold in the winter in church. Cool in summer despite the heat.

Breaking apart two dogs who are fighting?
Beating Keeper's face with your fists?
Suffering a wound when you attempt to feed a strange dog?

I get up early. I do the chores. There is always plenty to do around here. I read in the intervals – when I have time. I go for a daily walk on the moors – just me and the dog. Occasionally the others come along too, but they tend to dawdle. I like to keep things vigorous and brisk.

She had the care of four of the children of the family. She was to groom the three young daughters to catch a husband. The boy of the household was in need of some Latin and Greek. Her brilliant brother was losing some of his boyhood lustre. Her brilliant brother was taken on to teach the boy.

The world within \ unuttered harmony \ i could not speak \ loved thy living face \ the waste of years \ soul to feel the flesh \ on its surface seen \ my outward sense \ must be mine \ solacer of human cares.

High-backed, primitive, green-painted chairs.
A dog chasing a warbler in the heath.
A bitter whirl of wind and falling snow.

> *Love and hate equally / admittance into my own residence / take it as a gift from god / running red-hot needles into her / converted into a stranger / many things to be considered / the use of my creation / feared he would vanish / gathering elf-bolts / bring a tale to me.*

No matter. It is no matter. We are the rocks on which we stand.
Friends exchanging stories over cups of tea.

I would not go to heaven without Heathcliff – he would not go to hell without me. It looks like we are condemned to perpetual life. *Have such faith.* Oh Edgar, Edgar, Edgar. You have a brother – at last you have. Heathcliff will become another Linton. There will be four of us from now on. *Get accustomed to him.* We will throw a window open and we will sit and sip our tea and Heathcliff will gradually open up and talk about his adventures. He will tell us where he has been and what he has done. For you must agree, my darling Edgar, things can be very dull around here. To you the opening of a window is adventure enough – for me, it's as a child begins to breathe. *Take no revenge.* I have sat and said not a word, but I have often been quite miserable – miserable to wonder where my Heathcliff has taken himself. But I have been quite happy too, as you well know. Elated over and over again – when I would think of the exotic life he might well have led. Exotic India – far-off China – life in the wars or on the seas. Sails swelling and waves crashing on the other side of the world. *I'm an angel.* Oh you must see things as I can see them – you must look at life through my eyes. You will learn to love Heathcliff as I have done since we were both children out on the moors. And he, in turn, will come to love you as do I. He will tell us all his secrets – all of his dangers by flood and field. The three of us and Isabella. All of Heathcliff will now be ours as we sip our tea.

One day, the girl's eldest sister had an idea.

Torn the young girl by the ankle.
Been the book in which she writes.
Been the broken pane
on which the blood runs down.

I sud more likker look for th' horse. It 'ud be tuh more sense. Bud aw can look for norther horse nur man of a neeght loike this – as black as t' chimbley! Und Heathcliff's noan t' chap tuh coom at maw whistle – happen he'll be less hard o' hearing wi' ye!'

The angels seize me again by the arms! Their fingers bite into my flesh! I struggle to look through the cloud! The cloud grows dense and white and whispy! I see shapes but cannot see faces! I give a mighty pull! I pull the angels off their balance! They seize me again in a vice-like grip! They nod to each other and fling me down below! Now I float somewhere in the clouds! Somewhere between the earth and the heavens! I wonder what is going on below!

A whole new existence - choose another chapter - all turned to enemies - a very large stone - led me to his altar - wolf about to spring - we unbar the door - yah's see, all on ye - blows with force - meeting on the heath.

I used to lie on my bed at night! I used to wonder what was wrong! I would blow the candle out and try to sleep!

My teeth would chatter in my jaw! My heart would rise up out of my chest! My feet would twitch as they were running out on the moors!

Which was life and which was dream? In the morning Nelly would bring me a cup of tea! Beside the bed my silken slippers would be in shreds!

Negotiations dragged on forever.
Eternity shows no respect for time.
St. Peter was cautious but optimistic.
The devil certain that he would have the advantage this time.

A contretemps with Isabella. She is the mouse who has not been noticed. Suddenly she is on her hind legs and roaring in pain.
A new-born lamb staggering towards a slavering wolf.
Who would think that meek Isabella would want a life? Blonde hair – white skin – dainty elegance. A lapdog in her looks and in her mein. Quick to anger if she doesn't get a treat. She has been quite cross of late. Now the cause is out in the open. She has grown quite fond of Heathcliff. Will wonders never cease? *An arid wilderness.* Heathcliff the wild – Heathcliff the untamed – Heathcliff the whinstone and the furze. This is absurd, Isabella. Don't you see how fragile you are? Of no more strength than a sparrow's egg? Would a canary seek the moors on a winter's day? *Fierce, pitiless, wolfish.* Can't you see he's a wolf in the forest? – sniffing the wind and eyeing the fold? He will pluck your fingernails out and black your eyes. Oh so I am selfish am I? A dog in the manger? – a hoarder of gold? I am the one who covets the diamond – covets the pearl? *He'd crush you.* I have done with Christian charity. I release the infernal powers. Very well then, Isabella – from now on, every child must save itself.

The young master tries to drive the two children apart.

Overjoyed to have my soul united again.
Making plans for Edgar and Heathcliff and me.

A raging fire burns within me! A fire must burn – I am sure – in his breast as well! But why does he say so little? – why so seldom solicit my thoughts! Oh, why has he so forsaken me? Would that I could only afford to take extra lessons! To hear the French authors from his lips! His wife stands firmly be-tween us! – she disapproves of my every thought! She is mundane! She is sti-fling! She is cramping his every thought! She does not know the great depths inside him! She does not know how his soul yearns to soar! Oh, I know I have made a grave error! I gave him an inkling of how I feel! But how hide such fire and such passion! These are waves that one cannot conceal! They wash over one in the most mundane of encounters! They become the visible image in one's eyes! We used to spend much time at our lessons! He taught me how to read and write! Now he assigns me to teach when he is at leisure! Now he teaches when I have time to spend with him! Things are not as once they were! Did we talk for hours or does memory just make it so?

Intense the agony - take it or leave it - she splashed and giggled - tries to look through - regular letting of blood - never get a choice - crushes every rock and flower - if i were in your place - a path of dust and dung - decipher her faded hieroglyphics.

Meet me at midnight, Heathcliff! I conjure you to appear! Meet me at the churchyard after dark!

We must talk and talk and talk! The Heights and Grange gossip of twenty years! You must tell me everything that has transpired since I have been gone!

I want every detail of every encounter with those that I have loved! Surely my death has meant for something! Surely grief for me has made you all as one!

"You have worked so hard for this boon," says the Queen of the Faeries.
"Present yourself at the faery clock at one minute to twelve.
Every wish you have will come true for the rest of your life."

Heathcliff and Isabella in the library. I bring this to a head. I have some-thing I want to say and that I will do.

A woman telling the truth and not being heard.

I shall brook Isabella's sulking in silence no more. I shall show her that Heathcliff is under my sole command. He let the lapwings alone as soon as I gave him the word. *Physical and moral beauty.* Isabella tries to escape me – I stand between her and the door. You are so foolish Isabella – so much of life that you do not know. It is only I who protect you. Without my cape you'd be drenched in the storm. Do you not know what a force I am holding back? *Quarrelling like cats.* Is she not pathetic, Heathcliff? How dare she speak of love! The love that I bear for Edgar – the love that Edgar bears for me – the love that you and I have always had! Tell her what I have told her – tell her we two are in accord. How can she possibly imagine love on such massive scale? *Eternal oblivion.* Heathcliff – tell her that she is mistaken. Tell her that you are not interested in her. I command you to tell Isabella what she needs to know –

that your love is other-worldly – that you cannot love such as her – that man and wife has not a patch on the world we have known. *A strange repulsive animal.* Heathcliff seems to want to spare her – he seems to want me to let her go. I relax my hold for a moment. She digs her claws deep in my arm – a tigress inside a mouse. I release her and she goes running from the room.

"I had no more sense than to put it on the landing of the stairs, hoping it might be gone on the morrow."

> *Two children talk of heaven.*
> *They know of which they speak.*
> *Perhaps it is a memory.*
> *Perhaps they angels are.*
>
> *A boy looking through a window pane.*
> *A tyrant who grinds down his slaves.*
> *A young girl spitting at a waif.*
>
> *They blow upon the candle.*
> *They pull the blankets close.*
> *There are shadows at the window.*
> *A cold wind blows outside.*
>
> Are you as animal as Keeper?
> Is Keeper as human as are you?
> What could possibly be the link between your worlds?
>
> *A person listens at the doorway.*
> *She sighs at what she hears.*
> *Wish all were safe in heaven.*
> *Better there than here on earth.*

Alone at last with Heathcliff. Isabella has left in a huff. *An angel-child with a brand-new riding crop.* Myself as an angel – a ministering angel. Something I had never thought to be. An angel of kindness, peace and love. I stand here holding gunpowder in my hands. *Speaking the truth.* Heathcliff – a warning to you. You must leave this as it is. You are still inclined to bitterness. I must keep your reins in my hands. Edgar and Isabella are like children – easily distracted – easily confused. I wanted to show her just how foolish she has come to be. *Represented your failings.* She has created a massive world out of nothing at all. But you and I have an understanding – we have been one since we ran on the moors. You spared the lapwings at my request – you must see Isabella and Edgar as lapwings too. You must treat them I treat them – they are my own. *In a plain light.* Remember – Heathcliff – we are together. We are together until the end. Your goods are mine and my goods are yours. I give you Edgar and Isabella and any children that I might have. I deliver them into your hands. You are the vagabond no more. We two have a special bond, of course, that the others will never know, but I am bringing us all together. That is why I had you shake hands. *Seize and devour.* All animosities shall end – all petty hurts and misunderstandings – all selfishness and distress. I am an angel, come down from heaven – I stretch out my arms and take everyone in. *This neighbour's goods.* We will all live at peace in this kingdom – Wuthering Heights and Thrushcross Grange. *Dismiss the matter.* I weave a circle around us all. Edgar-Cathy – Isabella-Cathy – yes and Heathcliff-Cathy too. I am you and you are me; we are them and they are we. There is plenty of love for me and love for you.

Chapter 9

Heathcliff 4

Out on the moors for a good long walk today. Swarms of bees in the heather. Wild ducks flying overhead. One lone high-flying hawk in an updraft, circling endlessly. Hated to tear myself away. Keeper and I both wanted to stay. Home to chores and family chatter and so many other pressing things. Now the table, the paper, the pen and I am free.

A man with a very simple plan.

Waiting in the orchard at Thrushcross Grange. The plan is very simple. I will see Cathy – just see her once – nothing more. *Agreeable disappointment.* I will say very little. Since she is married now, there is nothing I wish to say. I only want to look upon her face once again. *Deep-set and singular.* I want her to see what I have become since she said it would degrade her to marry me. Perhaps she will still feel similar sentiments. I have clothes and money now – and I know which fork to use – but if it's breeding she values, then I am still a waif. *Remembered the eyes.* As for the second part of the plan, it is simple in the extreme: to face Hindley – and tell him exactly what I think – and shoot him dead. *A worldly visitor.* The third part is to simply shoot myself. *Really you.* So I will say very little. It will all be on her side. Idle chatter is not my forte. These are my thoughts of which there is nothing I wish to share. *No lights from within.* Here is Ellen with her apples. I have been watching her all this time. I shall meet her on the step and send my word. I shall present myself as a man from Gimmerton.

To be

A bitter whirlwind of suffocating snow.
A person reduced to his right place.

A waif who has lost her way on the moors.

a thorn craving alms

Would you say you are Ellen Dean?
Would you say you are Joseph as well?
Would you say that you are Hindley and Hareton too?

of the sun.

A woman profiled in miniature on a wall.
A piece of iron for weighing potatoes and hay.
A brass collar engraved with a name.

She greets me in the hall. The face of which I have dreamed for three long years.
A man asking a woman of her plans.
I have done the impossible. Made myself rich and somewhat refined. There is no one in the world – including you, Lady Catherine – who thought I could. *Where is she.* My hands in your hands! My cheek against your cheek! Let me look at you! Is that love or merely surprise I see in those eyes? *Needn't be so disturbed.* I was not surprised to hear that you were married. The thought was always a constant pain which prodded my heart. *How will she take it.* I pictured Edgar falling off his horse and spitting his head wide open on a rock. Bright red would be the colour of the stream. Of course the kind of horse that Edgar would ride would never dare jump a fence or chance a ford. *Put her out of her head.* All I had were fantasies. When I was exhausted – wits'end – resources depleted – barely the energy to breathe – I would look deep into the fire and dream my dreams. *No comprehending it.* Oh how I've missed you since you've been away! Edgar gets tired of me speaking of you! Let me look at you – a new Heathcliff from top to toe! *I'm in hell.* So you are glad to have me back? Back to what, if I may so ask? What are your plans for me now that I have turned up at your door?

He stayed in his room – he moaned and slept. Spent his evenings at the Black Bull tavern. Bullied a shilling from his father. Treated the fellows to a round of cheer. Come the night the lad had nowhere to go but home.

"I wonder you should select the thick of a snow-storm to ramble about in. Do you know that you run a risk of being lost in the marshes?"

No air, no land, no water! No form of any kind! The void that all the Christians talk about! I am knee-deep in chaos! A black muck that sucks at my legs! Not a light to mark a horizon or a sky! Cathy beckoned to me and now I have lost my way!

An uplifting tale - what I don't know - one extreme tirade - until i know - cannot be damper or colder - whimper in his sleep - i have been desperate - people breed sorrows - eyes issue praise - maketh the book.

I could have left when your father died! But I could never have left you behind! So Hindley's cruelty had no importance for me!

Oh it was you – Cathy – you – who tempered my choler! Only for you did I keep my revenge on a leash! Only for you was I content to absorb the blows!

I was you and you were me! Every blow of Hindley's fist and every sting of Joseph's whip! Our one-ness softened every insult and every blow!

"I myself am in like predicament," said the other in reply.
"I too have a story to enact when I should arrive."

So why did she not show me in? Of course – it is not her house. She is asking permission from her master and her lord.

A ploughboy invited into the grande salon.

I am waiting on the stair – not below as she bid me do. I can hear every word that the two of them are saying. *Lifted the latch.* I hear the word servant – I hear the word ploughboy – I hear the word kitchen. I hear their little spat about the higher and lower orders. Why do I not turn and walk away? *Have the candles lighted.* Ellen comes to bid me enter. She is surprised that I am so high up on the stair. I will never be welcome here. Edgar will always look down his nose. He is a Hindley without a backbone or a fist. *The wild green park.* Cathy meets me at the door. Your smile is as wide as all the world. A smile that you wouldn't want your master to see. You take my hand and walk me into the grande salon. *Old house was invisible.* Come say hello to Edgar. How nice to welcome me to your world. The three of us shall sit and sip our tea.

But the extraordinary man was a married man. It was a love that could never be. She suffered much – she suffered greatly. Who could describe the relentless agony? She felt condemned to spend the rest of her life alone.

Waiting in the orchard at Thrushcross Grange.
Sending Ellen in with a message for Cathy.

Is this the day before Creation? Is this the day after the Fall? Has everyone gone to hell or heaven and left me here? Well, let them all be saved or let them perish! Whatever their fate it is nothing to me! My course is set on one single star! If I can find Cathy this will be a heaven to me!

Blood is still warm and wet - a mutual immortality - what the poison - had

half a mind - reduced to his right place - all be saved - does not make an im-
pression - the thing to do - will not be for me - a little ice-cold hand.

I was hiding in the barn. The rain poured down and the wind was howling.
I could plainly hear your voice calling out to me.

"Heathcliff come back! I have been misunderstood! You have failed to
understand what I meant to say!"

I could see you through the cracks between the boards. You were standing in the downpour near the wall. I slipped out and made my way across the
fields.

When the princess reached the throne room
the frog was sitting on the throne.

Cathy takes hold of Edgar's hand. She puts his hand in mine. I have half a
mind to crush his delicate bones.
A magistrate and a ploughboy shaking hands.
So you and I are the local gentry. Your disdain is quite apparent. We have
arrived here by different routes. How many throats did I cut, do you think, as
I climbed these stairs? *Looked wondrously peaceful.* I remove my hand from
his. He is frozen as if by a snake. He looks me up and down in a mood of dis-
may. *I shrank reluctantly.* I suppose you have a library. I remember you as fond
of books. I heard Cathy say it made you attractive to her. *What does he want.*
Yes ploughboys can dress well too. They can also acquire great wealth. Feel
free to look me over as long as you please. *Recalling old times.* I'm sure that
your books are full of ideas. Cathy once told me that I had nothing of interest
to say. *A cordial reception.* The weather – the roads – sending Nelly to fetch
some tea. Edgar grows pale as we sit and talk. Perhaps remembering the gift of
the hot tureen. *Gaze fixed on him.* I am sure you shut yourself in your library
while the sun shines on the heath or when the wind and the rain jolt the countryside alive. Turn your page and sip your tea while the world goes on despite
you. *Feared he would vanish.* Your welcome is noted, Edgar. I'll make my
visits frequent ones. Every day there will be less air for you to breathe.

A breeze blowing through the moorland grass.
Guide-stones covered in snow.
A boy whose name is carved above a doorway.

Plain food – that's all we need. A joint of meat – carrots, potatoes. Milk-
and-rice pudding. Spice cake, drippings, tripe. On special occasions, a pie.
Every Brontë always has enough to eat.

Are all of these people living alone?
Does each of them dwell in a separate space?

Does each of them move through life in silent agony?

Oh, the peeling of the potatoes – the baking of the bread. These are necessities of the surface. What one must do to stay alive. Walking on carpet and forgetting the rock beneath. I guess I am best when I am alone. That is when I am most myself. I judge other people by how well they leave me be. No other person has ever entered my private realm.

It was to her a less than satisfying position. However, she set her chin and fixed her mind. She schooled herself to endure the petty slights. She kept her disapproval under wraps. She won the admiration of the girls.

Could never dream \ i had hoped to sing \ prize my memory \ neath stormy blasts bending \ spirit wandering wide \ flesh to feel the chain \ the music ceased \ my inward essence \ far, far removed \ my present eternity.

The feathery flakes of a snow-shower.
Poems kept away from prying eyes.
Large and small names scratched into paint.

Bestow my own attributes / private manner of interpreting / vain weather-cocks are we / clinging to the ledge / to adopt a double character / your own flesh and blood / entirely contained here / is it really you / full of little skeletons / a mere ruin of humanity.

I sit on your velvet furniture. I look around the room. He has made your life as barren as his own. Picture you two running barefoot on the heath!
Two people thinking as they meet eye to eye.
So you step across the rug – so you take my hands again – so you laugh as if you are happy. How do you breathe the air in here? *Undisguised delight.* What do you talk about? – what could you possibly talk about? What could the two of you have to say that is any concern? *Their mutual joy.* So you shall think it a dream tomorrow – so you shall not be able to believe – so you have seen and touched and spoken to me once again. *One beside herself.* Whether the tea is warm or is cold? – the antics of Edgar's sister's dog? – whether the peasants need more discipline and less gruel? *Think it a dream.* So you chide me for running away – so I don't deserve this welcome – so the agony, you say, has been all on one side? Can you really believe that I never thought of you?

Each of the three sisters would write a novel.

What do they want from me –
these people?
What are the wounds

that cry out to be healed?

"Nay, nay, he's noan at Gimmerton! I's niver wonder but he's at t' bothom of a bog-hoile. This visitation worn't for nowt, and I wod hev' ye to look out, Miss – ah muh be t' next."

I am sinking down into chaos! Being swallowed by a bog! Somewhere between the Heights and the Grange! Surely Cathy has left some markers! She is somewhere on these moors! Many times we romped in the moonlight! Not a sliver of moonlight now! Cathy – I know you are somewhere near me! Why do you torture your old companion? Teach me how to read your markers in the dark!

To see what must be - prefer to have no audience - to face his wrath - living in a dream - always wipe his hands - writing materials strewn - embrace of life and death - a family at odds - covers up the valleys - drive him out of his heead - write the third.

I came into the room. They were fighting over Hareton. Hindley was threatening to make Ellen swallow a butcher knife.

He was the child of Hindley Earnshaw. He was heir to Wuthering Heights. Whenever I looked at him, Cathy, I could see your eyes.

The boy dropped into my arms. I thought of bashing out his brains. Ellen cried out and I put the boy down on the floor.

Rules for entrance, rules for expulsion.
Rules for good conduct, rules for bad.
Rules for punishment and, in heaven, rules for reward.
Even rules for how to conduct a prisoner-exchange.

So you have suffered, have you, Cathy? – more than I could possibly have done? Is that what you have waited three years to say?

A man with a quiet smile and a raging mind.

You have welcomed me – kissed me – hugged me. Forced your husband to shake my hand. Do you think that this makes up for all you have done? *Prevent the law.* Do you remember things as I remember them? You were in the kitchen – dressed in your fancy gown. You asked why I was not outside – in the fields. I told you that Joseph was gone to fetch lime and that I was therefore free from my chains and we could go out on the moors and spend the day. And you said you didn't know whether Edgar and his sister would care to call. *Doing execution.* Beware of meeting me with a lesser greeting next time! I am aware of your shallow caprices! You shall have less luck in driving me off next time! *Out of mind.* You didn't look me in the eye. You knew these two were invited to call. You were building a wall between us, Cathy – a wall to shut me out. *There was cause.* If you had known the bitter life I have led you would not be so glib in admonishment! I waded through hell up to my chin for three long years! Every breath was a struggle and every breath was for you! *Striving to preserve.* You were picturing yourself riding in carriages – nodding to the peasants as you pass! You were picturing yourself sipping tea with this simpering fool in this very room! And picturing me – no doubt – pitching manure in Milady's barn! How can I trust – Milady – a single word that you say?

The two young children escape to the moors on a wind-swept night.

Seeing Cathy face to face after three long years.
Taking tea with Edgar's wife at Thrushcross Grange.

A chance for a new and fresh resolve. I was not cut out for young children. My dismissal almost came to me as relief. But soon – at Thorp Green – I shall have an ideal situation – the raising of two young and impressionable minds. The education of two young ladies – I relish the challenge of the task. Yes I shall train them in the ways of social necessity – a little French, a little German, some music, some singing and fancy-work. Drawing and dancing and social manners – enough to win them a man, at the least. All of this as parental requirement – understood, yes understood – but I shall see it as a vantage point – a situation in which I am placed – which shall allow me to tend the souls of my two young charges – to work for their betterment and their good. These are not children of five and six – these are young ladies of fifteen and sixteen. If I can set them on a path on which they will walk for the rest of their lives, I shall be grateful for having been summoned to Thorp Green. Where I have failed, I will succeed – enhance my strengths and diminish my shortcomings. I shall be the best Anne Brontë I am able to be.

A hand stirring tadpoles - if I were a different me - could live your life over - just two ghosts - my losses and gains - this purgatory end - write my story in the margins - nest beneath the throne - come out of your books - the world-the globe-the earth.

You moved on down the road quite quickly! Your life with me was very brief! A lightening flash and there you were and then you were gone!

Do you remember that day when Edgar – and his sister – came to call? And you were lingering in the kitchen? And I kept trying to get you to come out with me into the fields?

What were you thinking, Cathy? What were you thinking then? Until that moment I thought we were minds of a single thought!

Quite exhausted from the climb up the faery mountain.
Eyelids drooping from the long exhausting climb.

Looking around for a place to catch a wink or two.

Tea time without any tea. I sit and do not sip – Cathy sits and doesn't sip – Edgar sits and doesn't sip. Edgar's sister might sip or not – no thought for her. *A man obsessed by images from the past.* I fill them in on the new arrangements at the Heights. Cathy seems to sense no ill – Edgar bridles as I talk. Can you not believe that Hindley would invite me in? *Summoned by the bell.* And what of you, my brother Edgar? How polite you are striving to be. Are you remembering the hot tureen of applesauce which I hurled at your person? Perhaps that act will seem a trifle to you some day. *The meal hardly endured.* Memory is short for all but me. Cathy forgets that she drove me away – Hindley forgets his misdeeds of the past – even Joseph sees no need to be on his guard. *Cup was never filled.* Well I shall show you all someday. Every one of you has poisoned the well. You shall sip your fill of the brew I concoct for you. *Neither eat nor drink.* I cut the chatter short and express my regrets that I cannot stay.

"Miss Cathy and he were now very thick, but Hindley hated him, and to say the truth, I did the same."

A boy lies in an alleyway.
He has no thing to eat.
He begged upon the corner.
All the folk were poor as he.

A boy felled by the blow of a heavy weight.
An army marching against a colony of mice.
Pirates attacking a royal ship.

His stomach aches with hunger.
He finally falls asleep.
He dreams of kings and emperors.
Of princesses and queens.

Is each of them living a separate story?
Does each of them have a tale to tell?
How many unwritten novels are lost in these lives?

His eye is quick to open.
Hostile dog or hungry rat?
A man looks down at the urchin.
In his hands are bread and drink.

Walking back to Wuthering Heights. Walking up the familiar road. As a boy I walked this way one night in the dark.

A man who makes plans for the neighbourhood.

My plan for Hindley is running on apace – my plan for Hareton as well. I have both of them rolling precipitously down the hill. *Mischief under a cloak.* Her brother and her nephew – but what of that? Cathy never visits the Heights – she expresses no compassion for either one. *The bottom of my heart.* Cathy will never understand – we shall never see eye to eye. I tried to show her with the lapwings. Her love for me will protect her and no one else. *Better have remained away.* I'll keep my eye on Thrushcross Grange. It is not her natural home. I shall enjoy my role of master of Wuthering Heights. I look forward to the day when she shall return.

Chapter 10

Cathy 5

I prefer the kitchen and the baking. Charlotte prefers making the beds and cleaning the floor. Division of labour – the work gets done. I empty out the slops and sit down to write.

A woman with a very simple plan.

Peace and harmony – harmony and peace. These words have such a gentle sound. I am the glue that makes the joinery. We shall have unity as long as I am around. *Meditating on these things.* We shall sit here in the parlour – Edgar and Heathcliff and me. We shall go for long walks on the moors – call for the horses and take a ride. And Isabella, if she wants to come along. *As fresh as reality.* I have a gift, I think, for harmony. I have put Edgar in his place – I have put Heathcliff in his place – Isabella in her place. And even – I daresay – Ellen too. *A momentary belief.* Ellen is the slipperiest one of the rascals. But even with Ellen working against me, I have managed to smooth Edgar's feathers, I feel, though his patience is not without end. *Vanished in a twinkling.* With Heathcliff I must be quite blunt. Much has been altered by my marriage. Things were simpler when we were children out on the moors.

To be a person

A young man tying a cravat.
A boy hidden under a cloak.
Two lovers who swear a mutual curse.

learning to read

Why so painful to know other people?

What the poison and what the perfume?
Why have you chosen to live so completely alone?

one's own name.

A sampler carefully stitched with a Bible verse.
A powerful north wind blowing down a hill.
A girl with a figure lean and scant.

What is this – what is this? Ellen is muttering at the window. So what is taking place outside?
A woman and a man with clashing minds.
Is that Heathcliff and Isabella? He is offering her an embrace. What would cause him to do such a thing? I am enraged by the time that Heathcliff enters the room. *What are you about.* What is that smirk you have on your face? You are perplexing in the extreme! Why endanger our friendship in such a blatant way? Jealous of you? – how should I be jealous? – I have a husband of my own! *Draw the bolts against you.* Do you like her? Want to marry her? No – I know very well that you don't! You are a very foolish fellow! You are betraying yourself most of all! *Disregarded my request.* If you want to be barred from my presence, this is the way to go about it! Edgar will draw the bolts against you! You will never set foot in this house ever again! *Tell the truth.* You will be deprived of my company, if that means anything to you! If not then I have been all the more deceived!

He wasn't told that the girls were writing novels. It was felt that it would be painful for him to know. Night after night his sisters sat at the family table. They would hear him curse the dark when he came home. They didn't know what to think of him at all.

"He turned, as he spoke, a peculiar look in her direction; a look of hatred; unless he has a most perverse set of facial muscles that will not, like those of other people, interpret the language of his soul."

I am walking along a pathway! It takes me deep inside the moors! There is a green tree standing tall beside the path! There is a young girl in the tree! Sitting forlornly on a branch! It is almost as if I am seeing what once was myself! What I used to see in the mirror when I was a girl! All is still – not a sign of life! There is no breeze – there are no birds – there is not one note of song! Not the gurgle of water nor a hint of a wave in the grass! All is as dead as if she were lying in her grave!

Begins in a snowstorm - package it up - a great explosion - away from the light - a short history - dancing on the graves - a better place - a vicious blow

- and i am sure - does he not know.

It was the rebuff that left an impression! The corporeal hurt was nothing to me! And besides that encounter is no matter, for it is you, Heathcliff – you – who are the person I most earnestly want to see!

I have not had a moment's tranquility! Death has meant no peace for me! The agonies of life on earth have tortured me!

I float between the body and soul! I float between the head and the heart! Between my every deed and the throbbing memory-pain!

The prince and princess looked at each other.
Each was struck by the same idea.
Since neither could find their new kingdoms,
Would there be any harm in enacting a mixed faery-tale?

Scolding Heathcliff for his behavior. He says not a word as he moves over to the window. I bore into him again.

A woman attempting to calm two angry men.

Know you not that you are a guest at Edgar's indulgence? Know you not that he can withdraw your freedom to visit at any time? He says nothing to this logic and I exult in the assumption that he is listening and thinking as I do for now and for all time. *Every day I grow madder.* Shoes strike on the flagstones. Edgar hurriedly enters the kitchen. Has Ellen told him of Heathcliff's presence? I am sure that Isabella is not so inclined. *That blackguard.* Edgar stops and looks around. He looks from me to Heathcliff. He chooses to blame me for what he has heard. – that I have allowed this blackguard to use inappropriate language! – that I have suffered such abomination to be normal! – that I suppose that he – he! – saintly Edgar! – would stoop to such baseness too! *Habituated to his baseness.* Heathcliff stands his ground and sneers, and Edgar speaks as if he is speaking on my behalf! – that Heathcliff is miserable and degraded! – that he embodies a moral poison! – that he is contaminating me! – that he will hereafter be denied admission to our house! *Miserable degraded character.* How dare he speak in this way to our visitor!! He must see Heathcliff as an equal or the venture is lost! *A moral poison.* In response, Heathcliff decides to make things worse! – that my lamb has the ambitions of a bull! – that Heathcliff's knuckles will pay a visit to Edgar's head! Oh the two I love the most now most at odds! *Contaminate the most virtuous.* Heathcliff further sneers at Edgar! Edgar orders Ellen to fetch a pair of ruffians! Ellen turns away and makes towards the door!

Parted forever – forever parted. Deep waters in between. One heart – one head – one soul. Split asunder by the cruelty of the world. How to live without the air one needs to breathe?

Admonishing Heathcliff for his behaviour.
Disdaining Edgar for his thoughts.

There is someone else on the hillside! It is a boy and he is lying prone on the moor! He too is as still as death! No bees humming – no larks singing – no breeze whispering in the grass! It is cloudy and the sun is unable to shine! The boy does not move, as if he too is in a coffin! He too is waiting for sun and wind and song!

Waiting for twenty years - wastes beyond wastes - so completely alone - our initiatory step - lost her way - let them perish - the book of me - never a moment to oneself - i am your soul - called on to explain.

But you Heathcliff – you! You were the one I couldn't talk to! You were the one whose speech was studded with thorns and burrs!

We kicked the books into the dog-kennel! We roamed and rambled on the moors! But I wrote my story alone – in others' books!

There was no blank page for me! There was no blank page for you! But I dipped my pen in ink while the household snored.

Below the royal tower
the prince was lying prostrate on the ground.

Oh I have had it with these men! I slip ahead of Edgar and pull Ellen back inside the kitchen and slam and lock the inner-door!

A woman who insists on imposing her will.

Fair means! I cry – fair means! You are ruining everything I have tried to do! I want you both to stop and listen! *Courage to attack.* Edgar reaches towards my hand to seize the key! I quickly back away and turn to the fire and toss it in! Now I have you both in my keeping! No one leaves here until both of you shake hands! *Make an apology.* Edgar doesn't say a word but leans on a chair. I explain to him calmly that Heathcliff would never hurt him. He is a king who will protect us. He will act on my command. *Swallow the key.* Cheer up Edgar – as long as Heathcliff and I are friends, you never shall be hurt. *Flog you sick.* But Heathcliff ignores my gesture of silence! He moves towards Edgar's chair! He calls Edgar a milk-blooded coward! – He taunts him with his fist! – He calls him a slavering, shivering thing! He approaches Edgar as if he would give my husband a beating! He is giving the lie to everything I say! *Think an evil thought.* He kicks the chair on which Edgar is leaning! I attempt to get in between! I am about to calm them down. I am about to make my speech. I am about to make them friends. I have both of them subdued and locked in a room. Then Edgar seizes his chance to ruin my plan.

A beast prowling between sheep and fold.

Oat cakes steaming on a table.
Hieroglyphics in faded ink.

Different weather every day. Drizzling rain – brilliant sunshine. Green as grass – purple as heather – white as snow. A shawl will do quite well against the wind. Take a cape in case the weather takes a turn.

Who are these sisters who sit beside you?
Are you them and are they you?
Are they as far from you as the rest of the world outside?

Branwell is living, still, at home. He has been away, of course, from time to time. Something always brings him home, to us, again. His days are all pretty much the same. Sleeping late in the morning. Quiet, upstairs, in the afternoon. He barely eats anything and then off somewhere in the town. Later – a lot of noise as he comes back home. His life – as much as ours – is one of routine.

Then something went terribly wrong. Her older brother was dismissed from his post as a tutor. The experience was unpleasant in the extreme. A glimpse of human nature undreamt of til now. She resigned and returned to her home in acute distress.

Worlds of light \ the tempest's beating \ strike a tuneless string \ heaven laughs above \ dream tonight \ a child once more \ the noonday dream \ wings are almost free \ within this little frame \ that divinish anguish.

A line of upright stones daubed with lime.
Children's names chiseled on a gravestone.
Black chairs lurking in the shade.

Kept recurring and recurring / a range of gaunt thorns / decipher her faded hieroglyphics / uncomplaining as a lamb / nobody should let them in / what an infernal house / out of the common course / the great miseries of this world / struggled only for you / on the brink of the grave.

Edgar strikes him on the throat! Heathcliff was looking the other way – he was looking at me! Heathcliff puts his hand to his throat and tries to breathe!
A woman left alone in an empty room.
Edgar scurries past us both and out the kitchen door and into the yard. He will run around to the front and fetch some help. You'd better go! – all is ruined! – there's nothing now but for you to quickly go! *Wrest the key.* You are done with coming here! He will come back with a brace of men and with pistols too! You have ruined everything I have tried to do! *Hottest part of the fire.* Heathcliff threatens Edgar again! Can't you see that he is gone? He threatens

to murder him in this house! – to crush his ribs like a hazelnut! He expects me to stand and watch him beat Edgar down! Sounds on the flagstones outside! Two or three men are coming to take him! *We are vanquished.* They will have clubs! – they will beat you senseless! – you will never stand a chance! Do not stand and let them take you! – you must go now! *Played me an ill turn.* Heathcliff takes the poker from the fire, smashes the lock on the inner-door, and is through the door and gone and I am alone!

They would sit at the table and write.

Why should I be
locked in this garret?
Why should I run
free on these moors?

"Thank Hivin for all! All warks togither for gooid to them as is chozzen, and piked out fro' th' rubbidge! Yah knaw whet t' Scripture ses."

This girl is waiting for me! The boy awaits me too! Waiting for me to free the breezes! Waiting for me to un-snare the birds! Waiting for me to release the jubilee of song! She turns her eyes to me in question! I look around but I see no relief! There are no prisons out on the moors! No bars – no locks – no keys! What can I do to bring life to this waif who waits in the tree?

We correspond without speech - to get what I want - to judge another's worth - a thousand hammers beating - see death at work - fight like cats and dogs - she is not alone - flinging a girl - should I flatter myself.

What of Edgar? – what of Edgar? You were both the loves of my life! Did you reconcile after my death?
What of Hindley, my long-lost brother? Did he recover when I was gone? What did your sojourn at the Heights do for him – do for you?
What of Isabella too? Did she find a man to love? I left marks on her arm that time when I teased her of you!

Negotiations dragged on and on.
Finally they reached the final clause.
Now what to do with the girl and the boy?
The only two who had managed to dwell in neither locale.

I drag myself up to the parlour. I fling myself on the sofa. I am so agitated I cannot stand. Ellen accompanies me and I tell her all of my plan.
A woman sorting the fragments of her shattered hopes.
Tell Isabella to shun me – I blame her for starting this feud! It was for her

that I spoke to Heathcliff and now she is breaking up what was once a harmonious home! Her brother will never recover – and neither, Nelly, shall I – if Heathcliff should succeed in his devilish plan! *A thousand smiths' hammers.* Edgar is acting like such a fool! He was listening in at the doorway like a servant would do! I asked him – I begged him, Nelly – to leave Heathcliff strictly to me! I can control him, I said to Edgar! I am the one who Heathclilff always, always obeys! *Aggravate my anger.* And Heathcliff – foolish Heathcliff – why was he bound to talk in that way? I only wanted to question his designs on Isabella! – to tell him only love should be part of his plan! I would have encouraged their union if he had not said those things! Ellen's eyes I can see are against me, but I am bound to go on. *I shall get wild.* I scolded Heathcliff until I was hoarse. So why would Edgar turn on me? And then when they turned on each other, I knew it was the end! We have all been driven asunder for a long time to come! But I will no longer be the passive one! Ellen is silent but I know she opposes my plan. *Where we should end.* I am going to break their hearts Ellen! – break their hearts by breaking my own! You must tell Edgar that I am broken! – tell him my heart is cleft in twain! Tell him my health, you fear, is precarious, Nelly! – that my mind is running wild! A thousand hammers are beating in my head, Nelly! Tell Edgar of the frenzy that is attacking my brain!

They spy into the window of an elegant house.

Abandoned by Edgar and Heathcliff.
Deciding that I shall punish them both.

The Black Bull reels around me! All alone in the back room! A cursed cell in my private hell! On the rack of my shattered dreams for the rest of my life! My head upon the table! Drink after drink after drink! Keep them coming! Keep them coming! Just line them up right here and then leave me alone! Her husband dead! She in tears! The reading of the will! The inconceivable impediment! To be separated for life! Oh I could never have seen this coming! It has come as a thunderbolt! I had thought to take his place as lord and master! Her love for me was as slate or as granite! She a captive in her grand estate and me alone in my miserable one! In exile from my own heart's core! Condemned to live forever as a Haworth Cain! The dead hand of her vengeful husband held the will in front of her eyes! When she was told, she fainted hysterically onto the ground! My heart is squeezed to bursting! My life is one long tale of hopes withdrawn! Spilled ale! – a prince in exile! – a lost crown! I envy her that she is dying of her grief! I am cursedly robust! I shall be tortured on this earth for an eternity! I see nothing for myself but years of pain!

Scratched on the paint - these lost twenty years - we are listening - the best of human feeling - within a thin inch - things that make us cry - facade of wuthering heights - press you between the pages - splits the world in two - the lock on the inner door.

There is a burden on my shoulders! There are ropes around my wrists! If that is a knife you bear in your hands, then cut me free!

What is your purpose in coming to the window? Why do you call to me through the pane? Do you realize I've been lost for twenty years?

Can you tell me of my daughter? How has she fared these twenty years? I insist that you tell me everything you know!

Fast asleep beneath the magic-mountain clock tower.
Dreaming of wishes piled on wishes piled on dreams.
Fast asleep with eyes shut tight as the clock strikes twelve.

I am sitting in the parlour. I have lost the best part of my life. Edgar the cad comes up the stairs as cold as ice.

A frenzied woman with blood upon her lips.

He demands to know my intentions – will it be Heathcliff or will it be he? I admonish him most severely! How can you speak to me in icy tones when my own blood is boiling hot? *Hear no more of it.* I gave you my hand, but not my mind! I gave you my heart, but not my soul! Can I keep nothing for myself? Who are you to take my life and break it in two? *Your cold blood.* I demand to be left alone! I order him out of my sight! When he doesn't leave, I ring for Nelly! I fall down on the sofa, my head twitches and my teeth grind! Edgar mutters a word in my favour, but Nelly takes the floor! Ellen is turning her master against me! She is saying that I am a sham! I hear her telling him that I am pretending to be ill! *Worked into a fever.* I lie here in a frenzy! – I have blood upon my lips! – and he stands here listening to Nelly tell such lies! I start up! – I glare at the brazen traitor! Edgar says not a word in remorse or apology! There is ice in all his veins! I rush in panic to my room and slam the door!

"She had ways with her such as I never saw a child keep before; and she put all of us past our patience fifty times and oftener in a day."

Peasants working in the cornfield.
Take a break and have a drink.
There is one who brings the news.
One more bairn upon the earth.

Black eyes withdrawn suspiciously.
A mother who rejects an orphan child.
A poker smashing a lock on an inner-door.

What will be the path of this baby?
Will it be fate or will it be luck?

What determines the shade and the sunlight?
Is fortune given or ours to take?

Heard that Dickens lives with his characters?
Swarming around him as he writes?
Are Cathy and Heathcliff here, in this dining room?

Sing his ballad at the crib-side?
Scratch his tale on the coffin-lid?
Or will he be active in the grave-yard?
One of those still not at ease in eternity?

Alone! Completely alone! I lie here on the bed! All alone in this world and not one soul to care!
A woman all alone in a locked room.
All the bond I had with Heathcliff! – all the fondness I had with Edgar! Completely gone! *Senseless wicked rages.* They have turned against one another! Now they have turned against me as well! Wolves all! – wolves in the forest! – wolves in the fold! I tried my best to bring them together and this is my thanks! *Grinding her teeth.* Ellen offers to bring me breakfast. I have locked the door against her. How many days has it been? No! – always no! – I do not want to eat! If I am to be alone in this world then I do not wish to linger here! *The aspect of death.* I shall not answer to Ellen. I shall not answer to Edgar, should he appear. I have no desire to see Isabella ever again. *The aspect of death.* What was rock is now in fragments. Heathcliff has banished himself from my world. I am alone in an empty circle – completely alone. *Blood on her lips.* Satin pillows and satin sheets. I'd rather be lying out in a snowstorm. As cold and lonely as Wuthering Heights when I was a child.

Chapter 11

Heathcliff 5

Should I read this to Charlotte and Anne? They are willing enough to read their work to me. Perhaps I will – perhaps I won't. Perhaps I will choose another passage and let this one remain with me. They say that Dickens is inspired by the thought of his waiting readers. Emily-Cathy and Emily-Heathcliff – the two of us and no one else. We prefer to have no audience at all.

A person who is being closely watched.

Watching Edgar's sister in the court. She does not yet know I am here. I have been watching her feed the pigeons. I am waiting for something to happen before I approach. *Judas. Traitor.* A face appears at the kitchen window. Well, Nelly will have to do. I cannot wait here all day to get what I want. At any rate, the news will travel fast. I would wager a thousand pounds that Nelly will call her mistress to the window to see what she sees. If not then it will surely be conveyed – at first convenience – to her mistress as the pressing news of the day. *Hypocrite.* I approach Edgar's sister. She starts and turns away. I step across the pavement and ask her why she would shun my presence, as we find ourselves together on such a fine day. *Deliberate deceiver.* She hesitates for a moment and I place my hand on her arm. She has her face averted. She is looking down at the ground. She is never going to answer, the silly thing. Just as well, for I would hate to have to look at those Linton eyes. *Worthless friend.* I glance at the kitchen window again. Yes – Nelly is gathering news. I put my arm around Edgar's sister. – I whisper a few simpering words. I want to waste no more time than a moment or two. *Sneaking rascal.* I turn towards the kitchen as Edgar's sister turns away. It will be interesting to hear what Cathy will have to say.

To be

The cry of a desperate lapwing.
A visitor surrounded by snarling dogs.
A boy without a penny in his hand.

a red hot poker

Why such a vast cast of characters?
Why include Ellen and Lockwood and Joseph?
Edgar's sister and Hindley's wife?

searing tainted flesh.

A little lady reading aloud in the afternoon.
A house with a kitchen and a parlour.
A girl feeding pets with interesting names.

So Cathy has heard – Cathy has seen. I can see it in her eyes. They flash with all the life she had as a child.
A person telling another a few home truths.
Something about raising such a stir. Something about leaving Edgar's sister alone. *Insisted on silence.* Something about Edgar drawing the bolts, leaving me outside. Do you think five minutes of your attention is enough to last me for weeks and weeks? Is such the treasure of the unbolted door? *Your right place.* She takes her hand and wipes my brow. Clear your face of that bitter scowl! I restrain myself from brushing her hand away. *What are you about.* Something about offering the sister to me – as my wife. Do you like her? – do you like her? If you do you shall marry her! Mr. Linton will approve if I give him the word. *Draw the bolts.* Do you think that I'm your husband that you should be jealous of me? I am as free as any bird to build my nest wherever I please. Perhaps a few home-truths would help to clear the air.

All the brilliance of the morning – all the darkness of the night. The soaring of an eagle – a wounded bird in pathless flight. A fledgling falling from a nest as if a stone. As high as the mind can soar – as low as the body can crawl. He would lie there in the gutter and think his thoughts.

"This writing, however, was nothing but a name repeated in all kinds of characters large and small – Catherine Earnshaw, here and there varied to Catherine Heathcliff and then again to Catherine Linton."

I am in exile! I am in exile from myself! I am in search of the only existence where I can be free! I inch forward moment by moment! I inch forward in the dark! There is nothing that interests me along the way! I have no need for water or food! Netiher heat nor cold is repressive! I am a nothing who is in search of my only self!

Noises at the window - thinking silently - rain come pouring down - scramble out of the way - his right place - we walk on them - lost in the bog - high notions - a number of schemes - make my mark.

You did not see any value in me! You had me plain in front of you and yet you did not see! All you saw was a dirty ploughboy with workman's hands!

I was the mirror to your soul and you couldn't see it! All you could see were the fine clothes that the Lintons gave you! The Linton gift was a cover for your eyes!

If you had looked deep inside my eyes! If you had looked deep inside my soul! You would have found the very core of your truest self!

A very large stone
blocked
their path.

I don't want Edgar Linton's approval for anything I should do on this earth. His approbation is the last thing I should wish to attain. And as for marrying Edgar's sister – just you leave that decision to me. I shall take from him what I want without one word of please.

Two people standing out in the wind and the rain.

But perhaps a few words, Cathy – direct from me to you. A few thoughts of mine of which you should be aware. *Grinds down his slaves.* You are living in a nightmare, with velvet curtains and chandeliers! You are keeping a chamber in hell, where terrible deeds are done in your name! Every day the flesh is torn from off my bones! *Torture me to death.* I have suffered for you! – suffered! – and for that you offer a cup of tea! Oh, and a hand-shake, given reluctantly, from your lord! Yes I saw him wiping his hands as I left the room! *Levelled my palace.* And while we are speaking of protection – you are the only one I protect! You take a Springer for a guard-dog – better a wolf than a mass of warm hair! My revenge shall be to strip away the lies that your castle is made of! Think of me as a mighty storm and yourself as standing out on the heath! Your petty fancies will all break loose and blow away! *Erect a hovel.* When the wind dies down there will only be you and me!

One day the eldest sister had an idea. She and the two younger sisters would each write a novel. Each novel would provide one volume of a three-volume set. They would sit and write their novels at the family table. The three novels would help to pay the bills.

Meeting Edgar's sister in the garden.

Telling Cathy a few home truths.

I have been walking in the dark! There is no light of any kind! There seems to be flagstones under my feet! If I stray I will lose the path in grass or furze! But if I kneel and extend my hand there is nothing there! Do I keep to the flagstones? Do I strike out onto the fields? I have no idea where all of this will lead!

Aid was withdrawn - hard to look at her - send him away - i told the angels - measuring the gulf - the same idea - studded with thorns and burrs - two of us - something in your eyes - dream queer dreams.

We were dancing on the graves. You taught me to waltz, but I didn't want to. I stood and watched you as you conjured up the dead.

You were calling out to them. You knew some of them by name. You wanted to see them and to talk with them.

Why did you call on an ancient Hareton? Why did you call on a still-born Heathcliff? What did any of these dead ones mean to you?

God made
all his creatures.

Cathy turns on me like a vixen. Out in the open, I think for a moment. But to my disgust, she speaks with Edgar's voice.

A person who is perceived as something else.

Secure and tranquil! – secure and tranquil! This is the basis on which you want peace? So Edgar is best when even-tempered! So I am worst when I am me? *Ungrateful brute.* So I am the one inflicting misery? So I am the Satan in search of lost souls? And you and Edgar are ranged against me? – agents of tranquility? – agents of peace? *Treated you infernally.* Accused of inflicting misery! Given the name of ungrateful brute! And Edgar a saint who offers the gift of eternal peace! *Revenging yourself.* A new phase of character? – when I am a rock? You are the one who is no longer the child that you used to be! You are an Edgar – Cathy – an Edgar! A Linton through and through! And you can accuse me of betraying what it was we used to be?

An ash tree with blood upon the bark.
A person getting lost on a four-mile walk.
Every man's hand against his neighbour.

Primroses – snowdrops – daffodils. Crocuses poking their heads through snow. Water gurgling in the beck among the rocks. Moss gathering on the sides of the stepping stones.

Why two Heathcliffs and two Haretons?
Why the blacksmith and the boy with the sheep?
Who is even going to remember the doctor's name?

Charlotte spent more time in Belgium than did I. She went there, principally, to improve her French. The purpose was to prepare for the school that was to be established here at the parsonage. We never talk about Belgium. It meant different things to us both. It made a lasting impression on Charlotte. She still writes letters, I believe, to the people she met while she was there.

One day her eldest sister had an idea. She and the two younger sisters would each write a novel. Each novel would provide one volume of a three-volume set. They would sit and write their novels at the family table. The three novels would help to pay the bills.

Infinite immensity \ the word adieu \ t'is all in vain \ the spirit that remembers \ the unblessed of heaven \ always back returning \ thy phantom bliss \ its harbour found \ for the time \ the empty world.

Roads buried deep in fallen snow.
A painting with one figure erased.
An old man sitting quietly in the chimney-corner.

Shrunk icily into myself / talking nonsense by the hour / we should have peace now / she was half silly / she's out of her head / an echo of curses / my great thought in living / like one beside herself / all turned to enemies / it shall remain forever.

Edgar enters into the kitchen. I stand ready to face his wrath. A humming bird or a chickadee in an angry mood.
A person presuming to judge another's worth.
But so cowardly is Edgar that he pretends not to notice me, and squeals and squeaks at Cathy instead of me. *Habituated to his baseness.* Something about notions of propriety. Something about the language that I use in his house. *Carelessness and contempt.* Something about me being base and a blackguard and he being white as snow. Something about he and his house being soiled by association with me. *Miserable degraded character.* And he blames all this on Cathy – as if she has control over me. *A moral poison.* I move forward and stand between them. I am coiled and ready to pounce.

One sister sat to the left of her.

I have cried on
both sides of this membrane.

*Much from me has
been concealed.*

"Running after t' lads, as usuald! If I war yah, maister, I'd just slam t' boards i' their faces all on 'em, gentle and simple! Never a day ut yah're off, but yon cat o' Linton comes sneaking hither; and Miss Nelly, shoo's a fine lass! shoo sits watching for ye i' t' kitchen; and as yah're in at one door, he's out at t'other; and, then, wer grand lady goes a-courting of her side!"

I am pressing against a membrane! It is so thin I can feel it moving in and out! I lean forward and press my cheek! I stretch my arms and spread my palms! I can faintly hear a heartbeat from the other side! Once in awhile I feel a breath upon my cheek! It is dark so my eyes are without a significant function! I've been walking for years and years to get to this place!

A thorn craving alms - this will be a heaven - see no meaning at all - thought followed thought - you are my soul - all animosities shall end - have a secret language - shun my presence - ready to pounce - strip away the lies.

The fire was warm in the hearth. You were leaning against your father. My head was in your lap.

You went to kiss him. He didn't move. You called out that he was dead.

Joseph sent us to this room. You spoke so beautifully of heaven. I was thinking that now there was only you and me.

*Me you sky above.
What care me you?
Me you rock beneath.
What care you I?*

That he would speak to Cathy like this. That he would treat her as he does. I have never heard him talk to his servants this way.

Three people locked in a room without a key.

Well I have had enough of this. I will make him beg for his life. I will thrash him until he begs me to stay my hand. *Milk-blooded coward.* Before I can move to do so, Cathy bolts the door. He tries to take the key from her but her strength is more than his, and she throws the key in the fire and he slumps away. *Preferred to me.* He leans on a chair and trembles as I advance to give him his due. I pour out a flood of words as I roll up my sleeves. *Strike him with my fist.* Something of bulls posing as lambs. Something of cowards with milk for blood. *Kick him with my foot.* Something of slavering shivering things. Something of splitting his skull with my knuckles. Something of kicking him like the lap-dog he seems to be. *Faint for fear.* I give the chair an gentle push and turn to Cathy. I want her to see what her choice has been. She has chosen to set up house in a mouse's liar.

A watch-dog seizes the young girl by the ankle.

Feeling the urge to crush Edgar's skull like a rotten egg.
Walking back to Wuthering Heights in a towering rage.

The seagulls circle and dive above us! England is at hand! I dread going back to Haworth! I shall never see Belgium again! Once to love is once to taste of heaven! Once to lose is to never love again! Emily pealing those endless potatoes! Tabby rubbing her back in pain! Reading to Father in the lamp-light! Anne quietly doing her needlework! Branwell stumbling in at the door! I was born to live in Paris! An elegant robe and a coach and four! To tour the capitals of Europe! To meet the famous and chat of Voltaire! To travel south to where everything flourishes so, in the sun! Oh, why was he born a Papist? Why did he marry in his youth? Why so stern when my secret became so plain in my eyes? No I cannot blame his wife! So cruel and perhaps so kind! No, I cannot see myself as one who would share! Even one moment of reciprocal joy would be stolen from me! They are tying us up at the jetty! Dull clouds and the prospect of rain! Every year another birthday! How many years do I have before me? How many pebbles stretching out on an endless road? There is nothing for me in Haworth! I dread to put my foot on English soil again!

Did you set the trap - how little we used to say - never come true - a companion in her misery - peering in a window - a granite block - all i have to say - you have ruined everything - let me tell you clearly - adopt a double character.

Oh I would still degrade you now! I am Heathcliff now – I was Heathcliff then! There has been no Heathcliff 1 and Heathcliff 2!
You wanted to smuggle me into Edgar's house! Leave the kitchen door unlatched! Edgar saw me with Hindley's eyes – and you did too!
Who will you choose in heaven, Cathy? – that worm, Linton, or your self-soul – me? Hell is not a place underground Cathy! It is to dwell in the clouds of heaven – unloved by you!

The judge was
quite perplexed.
The case
could not proceed.

Edgar catches me full on the throat! I grab at my wind-pipe and try to breathe! I haven't endured a such a blow since I was a boy!
A man who imagines himself as a fiend in a towering rage.
My gullet burns like the fires of hell! He has done himself a bad turn! This

mouse has given me leave to thrash him like a man! *By hell.* So he has escaped by the outer-door! I will be after him at once! I will catch him in the courtyard and thrash the milk-toast until he pukes! I will crack his skull against the garden wall! *Crush his ribs.* I will leave Catherine with an invalid to tend – his body as feeble as his mind! *A rotten hazel-nut.* Dare to hit me and run away! Call me an fiend and run away! Leave your wife with a fiend in your scramble to save yourself! *Murder him.* I will take this poker and stuff it down his throat!

"From the hour she came down-stairs till the hour she went to bed, we had not a minute's security that she wouldn't be in mischief."

There are ghosts among the living.
Walk among us day by day.
Cannot see them; cannot hear them.
Cannot know who they may be.

A prince who is lost and rescued and lost again.
A boy falling from a banister.
A bell that breaks with excessive ringing.

They are searching – always searching.
There is something they yearn to know.
Their eyes they look quite through us.
We are the ghosts and they are the real.

Why not cut these people from the book?
Be as ruthless as Cathy and Heathcliff?
Do they not urge you to focus on just they two?

Why can they not leave earth behind?
Why was death not a welcome birth?
What did they lose while they were living
Mid the flowers and the filth?

Cathy catches me by the arm. She insists that I take my leave. Nelly too urges me to let the fellow go.
A law-abiding citizen smashing a lock.
He shall not come back alone! He shall bring ruffians – two or three! *The coachman.* I dare not go outside the law. I want all to be by the rules. I want to dominate Edgar by only lawful means. *Two gardeners.* I take the poker and smash the lock. A simple matter of slipping away. I shall make my escape by the inner-door. *Smashed the lock.* I turn and look at Cathy. I have a craving for Edgar's blood. I glare at her and then I turn and take my leave. *Made his escape.* Cathy calls to me as I leave. Something about no longer being welcome at Edgar's house.

Chapter 12

Cathy 6

Help Tabby with the fire – she's getting old. Help Charlotte with the ink – there's plenty left. Help Anne with the paper – on the shelf. Leave the latch unlatched for Branwell. Check the animals for water and for food. Now sit down and dip the pen and maketh the book.

A woman who is starving at a feast.

Undoing the latch and unbarring the door! Parched! Parched! Parched! More water – Nelly, please! *One sensible soul.* But before you go, I must ask you a thing or two! Where is that creature, Edgar? No doubt he and that creature, Heathcliff, are both lying dead of their foolish duel on the parlour floor! Where has Edgar been all this time, Nelly? Has Heathcliff even once come to call? *Believed no such thing.* At his books? You say at his books? Shut up in his study all this time? Does he not know I am on the brink? *Kept it to myself.* Tell him I'm dying here of hunger! Tell him to get his nose out of those books! *Strange exaggerated manner.* Does he not know that I am dying? – that his indifference is the knife that is probing my heart? Tell Edgar that my life is in grave danger! And if Heathcliff should come to call – send him away!

To be

A wayfarer fallen into a snowdrift.
Eggs lying helpless in a nest.
A handsome, rich, dull marriage prospect.

a pathway hidden by drifts

Hiding with Cathy in the faery cave?

Stalking with Heathcliff for helpless birds?
Living and breathing with these people every day?

of pure white snow.

An ancient story being told in a Yorkshire brogue.
Hard, black frost on a bleak hilltop.
A drawing of a girl alone in her room.

Is that Catherine Linton, Nelly? That face in the mirror there? It is ghastly, as if a ghost has taken my place!
A woman who attempts to efface herself.
Oh I am dying and no one cares! Look! – look close at the mirror, Nelly! This is what Edgar must be brought here to see! He would see if he would deign, once, to glance up from his books! *Her true condition.* Oh, he locks himself in his library, Nelly! I tried the door, once or twice in the night, but I had no key! No one cares what I want, do they Nelly? – what I want out of all this? *Acted a part.* I thought that though everyone hated and despised each other, they could not avoid loving me! That they would all sup together for me – do you see! *How I'm altered.* Edgar has set himself against Heathcliff! Oh, I would surely kill myself if I could be persuaded that the loss of me would be an end of him! *Speaking the truth.* The sooner I die the better! They will both of them rue my loss! The sooner gone the sooner forgotten! I am sorry I ate that toast and drank that tea!

Why does the future not fulfil the promise of its origins? Why does the acorn not grow to a mighty oak? Why do flames turn to ashes in the grate? Why is the path through the bog so very narrow? Why does brilliance lie tarnished in the rain?

"An immediate interest kindled within me for the unknown Catherine and I began forthwith to decipher her faded hieroglyphics."

I am in the garden at Thrushcross Grange! I hear weeping but I cannot see anyone! This is where we used to walk on pleasant days! This is my favourite old ash-tree! Why there is blood upon the bark! It has trickled down and stained the ground below! Why is there so much blood upon this tree? Who is he who suffered here? Why is the blood still warm and wet after so many years?

Such a wretched thing - caused the loss - never a notion - we have been banished - all one needs - still holding the whip - looking through a pane - that dreadful boy - a book of poems - write on the margins.

I have been waiting for twenty years! At least twenty if not many more! Oh it has seemed an eternity to me!

I told the angels I would not go with them – I shrugged them off and retained my place! I could not live without those I loved – whether in heaven or in hell! Any place but my home would be repugnant to me!

I had hoped I could watch and listen, but that was a comfort which was denied! I have been kept as if in a prison – no knowledge nor power, but only hope! I waited and wondered and hoped against hope for all to be well with those who remained behind – alive!

They both agreed
that the stone
should be removed.

Tearing the pillow with my teeth! Pulling out feathers from the rents!
A waif who is lost in drifts of snow.
We have many pillows, Nelly! I have only peered into one! I only want to find what is hidden deep inside! Feathers of all kinds and colours! I toss a handful in the air and it floats to the floor! *Feverish bewilderment.* Snow is falling all around me! I am back at the Heights, I believe! – the middle of winter! – in only a nightgown! – the wind is blowing from the north-east! *Brought to my recollection.* Turkey, wild duck and pigeon! Moor-cock and lapwing – a bonny bird! Every feather, you know, Nelly, has something it wants to say! Every feather is whispering tales while we are asleep! *Ranging them on the sheet.* Oh why would you set a trap? Six little skeletons cold in their nest! And the mother lapwing helpless to give them their need! You should never have come between them! You must promise me, on your heart! *Other associations.* You must never shoot a lapwing ever again!

She asked herself what she could write about. Her own experiences were closest to her heart. She would write about the trials of a young pupil-teacher. What it was like to be abroad and attending school. About the difficulties of making one's way in the world.

Locking myself away in a room.
Refusing all earthly comfort or sustenance.

There is a man leaning over a bannister! It is the staircase at Wuthering Heights! I used to climb to my room to write on rainy days! He is holding a boy in his arms! He is cursing and his eyes are wild! He leans over and shakes the boy and lets him go! The boy is falling towards the flagstones! An infant is standing down below! The boy lands in his arms! The infant holds the boy as if he would smash him against the wall! I cry out but my voice is not heard! The infant hesitates and considers what to do! I cannot tell what he intends to do with the boy!

Value to the world - person from another world - a wayfarer fallen - a comfort which was denied - tries to look through - neither could find - all warks togither for gooid - ride in the dark - it was myself i saw - as fresh as reality.

And what of Hareton – Hareton Earnshaw? Such a majestic name and such a helpless little boy! He had only you and Hindley, as Ellen came to live with me!

Did you help Hareton to his legacy? You are his uncle, as you well know! Remember I showed you the name which is chiselled over the door?

I gave birth! – I know I gave birth! – I can feel the birth-pangs yet! Oh I know it was a daughter! – I have known it for twenty years! – I heard Ellen speak of a girl as I slipped away! Oh, you must tell me what became of my bonny bairn?

He smiled
when they were made.

Gather elf-bolts by yourself, Nelly! I shall stay here in my cave!
A touch of madness at the thought of coming years.
Why should I help you if you are going to hurt our heifers! Did you betray me every time I helped you before? *What you'll come to.* Fifty years hence, Nelly! – fifty years hence! What will become of all of us fifty years hence? I always think of twenty years as a very long time! *Not so now.* The snows will still drift deep in the winter! The rock will still be underfoot! The spring will change the leaves on the trees and they in turn will wither and die when their sap is gone! *I'm conscious it's night.* Grey hair, Nelly! – grey hair for you, but not for me! Bent over and gathering elf-bolts as you have done for years on end! Bent shoulders and a collar turned up against the cold! *I see a face.* I'll be the grass on which the goats and the heifers feed!

The imprints of fingers on an arm.
A tattered shoe lost in a bog.
Two children whispering in a garret.

Chores and Bible-reading. Sit by the fire and think one's thoughts. Peat, wood, coal. How many shapes can you possibly see in the shifting flames? Nine o'clock and the clock is wound and the day is mine.

Cathy and you at the stationer's shop?
Heathcliff smelling your cakes on the hob?
The two of them sitting among the Brontës as you dine?

Anne is the writer of us all. She tends to the ink and trims the pens. She sits down punctually at nine o'clock, after things have been cleared away. Always ready to share her thoughts. Always ready to read us a passage. Her novel seems to be moving along quite well. Never pauses – like Charlotte and I – to consider what next to write. Anne will prove to be the writer in the family some day.

She asked herself what she could write about. Her own experiences were closest to her heart. She would write about the trials of a young governess. What it is like to be neither servant nor gentry. About the difficulties of making one's way in the world.

A lip of cruel scorn \ rend another heart \ a mutual immortality \ years of change and suffering \ wastes beyond wastes \ those first feelings \ as they were life \ measuring the gulf \ without identity \ visions rise and change.

A book, a pen and a pot of ink.
A path with swamps and bogs on either side.
Stunted firs at the end of a house.

Retired colder and farther / worrying my brain / his soul's concerns / looks an out-and-outer / inward and outward repulsiveness / can't make yourself content / if all else perished / I'm an angel / never shoot a lapwing / her existence depended on that of another.

Asleep? Nay, I do not sleep! I have had not a wink of sleep since I began starving myself to death!
A mirror with a tale it wants to tell.
So who is that face in the mirror? Pray how can you tell that it is I? *The shawl had dropped.* If I were pressed to solve this puzzle, I would say that it is the me that once was me! *See yourself in it.* You will catch cold without your shawl, Nelly! The wind is cold and from the northeast! The room is haunted! I shall cover my eyes as well! *Trembling and bewildered.* Why do you say that it is nobody, Nelly? – why do you say that it is myself? What do they say is true when the clock is striking twelve? *My brain got confused.* Do you ever dream of dreams, Nelly? – ever dream of dreams of dreams? – dreams that surround and frame the dreams that we usually dream?

One sister sat to the right.

A river of black flows
through this landscape.
I lay down my
head on this rock.

"It's bonny behaviour, lurking amang t' fields, after twelve ut' night, wi' that fahl, flaysome divil of a gipsy, Heathcliff! They think Aw'm blind; but Aw'm noan: nowt ut t' soart! – Aw seed young Linton, boath coming and going, and Aw seed yah, yah gooid fur nowt, slattenly witch! nip up und bolt into th' hahs, t' minute yah heard t'maister's horse-fit clatter up t' road."

A young girl noses her pony up a hill! I regret that I cannot see her face! The wind blows strongly and the air is chill! It is a path that I used to know! I have been here many times! Heathcliff and I took this path to Thrushcross Grange! But that was many years ago! Why is she so determined? Why is she picking her way up the hill? What is she seeking? What does she need? Why can I not reach out and touch her? What will she find when she arrives at Wuthering Heights?

Revenge on a leash - failed to understand - all my loves - the ear begins to hear - always waiting - petty hurts and misunderstandings - silence at its core - interesting to hear - slam t' boards i' their faces - your petty fancies.

How many people in that antagonistic tangle I left behind? Oh Ellen! – bothersome Ellen! She saw herself as the shepherd of our lives!

And Joseph – what of Joseph? Irascible, self-righteous Joseph! No – with all his faults I cannot make any exceptions!

How have you lived with these people, Heathcliff? Surely my death has gone for something! Surely my death has made a circle where there was none!

Me you chandelier.
What care me you?
Me you window pane.
What care you I?

The wind is sounding in the furs by the lattice! It comes down straight over the moors! I am lying in my chamber at Wuthering Heights!

A person peering at a window in search of herself.

The casement is ajar! I am in my oak-panelled bed! My heart aches with some great grief! Hindley has just ordered a separation between Heathcliff and me! *Dreams appal me.* Lying alone for the first time! I have spent the night in weeping! I am only twelve years old, but my life has ended! I have a strange presentiment that I will be wrenched from here, at the Heights, and converted – at a stroke – into someone else! *A cold blast rushed through.* Wrenched from my all in all! Taken from Heathcliff for all of time! An exile and an outcast from my childhood world! *Subdued her spirit.* Oh I am dying, Nelly! – dying! I am groveling in an abyss! I am dying in this sickroom! *A wailing child.* I must have air or very soon I shall cease to breathe!

The young boy tries to pry open the slavering jaws.

Fearing madness at the end of all my years.
Finding a mirror and a window in my path.

Lying awake for a just a few minutes – as I do at the end of the day. Balancing out the ledger of my losses and gains here at Thorp Green. Trying not to let myself wallow in cynicism or despair. Sometimes I feel I shall be life-long friends with my two young charges – they come to me for advice and, at times, for prayer. At other times, I feel that I have been thrust among the pagans – where other lives are sacrificed, with no thought of the word of God or of common decency. To have strayed so far from the best of human feeling – to have had no pattern of love or kindness from those who should have been mindful to show the way – to trifle with the heart of another, for the rewards of a parlour game. To break a heart when one wouldn't damage a favourite toy. It will take every ounce of my influence to break that chain. And as for Branwell, I have no words. I cannot believe what he has become. Every day I witness moments in which I catch my breath in disbelief. I am slowly falling asleep. Every night I practice my speech of resignation. Yesterday I was asked to stay for two more years. I dare not speak my thoughts to Branwell. The mistress assumes that I shall stay. How can I leave here when I owe so much to these girls?

Watch yourself sip champagne - the most galling thoughts - without a word - I cannot speak - as harmless as sand - i'll be the madwoman - the life you have failed to live - tale of hopes withdrawn - a roof or a rainstorm - two people thinking.

How does my daughter, Heathcliff? How does the daughter to whom I gave birth? Why do you hesitate when I speak to you?
My daughter is my flesh and blood! I willed her into existence! She is the flesh I left behind when I left this life!
Of course my daughter has my eyes! Whose eyes would you expect her to have? My daughter is as much a part of me – as much me, myself – as are you!

The prosecution spoke
exclusively
in the language of apples.

Open the window Nelly! I'm burning up with the heat! Oh Nelly, how I wish that I were out of doors!
A candle burning in a room for twenty years.
Let me have some air! I must go out on the hillside! I wish to be a girl again! Half savage and hardy and free! I want to run again with Heathcliff

across the moors! *I had barred the door.* Open the casement, Nelly! Who would be so unkind as to close it? Fasten it open! – there's a dear! I am dying and you must give me a chance at life! *Utter blackness overwhelmed me.* Oh you are useless to me, Nelly! Must I do everything myself? Very well then! – very well! *No command of tongue.* I am up and across the room! Throwing it back! – bending out! – feeling the bite of the frosty air! The wind cuts across my shoulders, as keen as a knife! *He did not guess.* Not a moon! – misty darkness! – but I can see a candle-light! I can see Wuthering Heights from here! – I can see the candle shining in my room!

"Her spirits were always at high-water mark – her tongue always going – singing, laughing and plaguing everybody who would not do the same."

She is sane and she is sober.
Sees each moment for its worth.
Scrubs the pots and cooks the dinner.
Hangs the washing out to dry.

A man who is in love with a married woman.
A person who is given up for lost.
Veins filled with icy-water from a beck.

Why the angst and why the turmoil?
Why the agony and pain?
Leave the searching after fireflies.
Stir the pot upon the hob.

Rejected with Cathy at the gates of heaven?
Rejected with Heathcliff at the gates of hell?
Where will you and your characters go from here?

Take a walk when sun is shining.
Stay indoors when there is rain.
Who has time for mental journeys?
Someone has to bake the bread.

Yes I challenge you, my Heathcliff! You who stand before me now!
A child taunting another to follow a path.
I am asking you to venture! I do not want to live alone! I am asking you to walk with me, hand in hand! *Life grew a blank.* Remember how often we went to the churchyard? – telling the ghosts we had come to call? No velvet curtains there, nor chandeliers! *Memory burst in.* Go upstairs to my childhood bedroom! A candle is glowing, there, in the dark! The trees are swaying in the yard! Come to the window! – we'll meet at the window! *Temporary derange-*

ment. I'll not rest until you are with me! I shall be tapping on the glass! *An exile and outcast.* Oh – you need time to think it over? – you need time to consider your path? Forgive me for wondering at your sincerity! You have always followed me! – will you refuse to follow me now? *What had been my world.* I shall wait though it might take a hundred years!

Chapter 13

Heathcliff 6

About twice a week we exchange ideas. We each read a passage and there is always a comment or two. Once in a while I raise an objection -- most of the time I don't say a word. You write your novels and I will write mine -- that is all I have to say. Two of you and two of us – Keeper always agrees with me – so let us dip our pens in the ink and get on with the game.

A person awaiting her future in the dark.

Edgar's sister's room! A candle in the window! I give the signal for her to come down! No doubt she has made a fine selection from her trousseau! *Run of wi' her.* Rags will do you well enough, if you only knew! Your ride in the dark will not keep you as clean as a coach and four! *It cannot be.* We shall have a few hours head-start, but what of that? I could have collected her in daylight – she is of age and of eager consent! *How should we do.* I almost regret not seeing the look on Edgar's face! No doubt his breakfast a few hours from now will have a new and bitter taste! *Trouble me no more.* The whole house is dark and peaceful! The Grange dogs have learned to be friendly – it wasn't their way a few years ago! Does anyone dream of a thunderclap? No doubt Cathy lies in the bliss of contented sleep!

To be

A mother who dies while still a child.
Writings hidden away from prying eyes.
The first lady in the neighbourhood.

a lapwing trapped within

What is a poem and what is a novel?
What can each reveal and conceal?
Which of the two is the ideal Emily-form?

a nest.

A painting which fails to capture its subject.
A tall girl with fair hair and interesting eyes.
A girl playing Beethoven on a piano.

So this is Fanny is it? – your Springer? She would be breakfast for the wolves at Wuthering Heights! Well, we shall hang her here suspended, for all the world to see! A message that I couldn't write better with pen and ink! You must leave this world behind you – best to face that fact right now! You shall see what it shall be to be torn away from your former self! You shall not be the person you were in a fortnight or two! I'll take this handkerchief, Milady – you won't be needing it at the Heights! It will do to collar your handful of yappy hair! Perhaps her yelps will wake the inhabitants of the house!

Two children whose souls merged into one.

Well Cathy – look at us now. You plucked us apart at twelve years old and we have both of us suffered alone from that moment on. Your present state is self-inflicted – yes it is, though you don't dare to say. You have been your own worst self through all these years. *I'd give the world.* And you have forced me to be a Cathy – though I have fought every inch of the way. Whatever you say of me I would double-say of you. You are with Edgar – stifling Edgar – who snuffs out all that is best in you. And I am here – with Edgar's sister – a hated Linton – because of you. *My heart returned.* I should have run away after your father brought me home, hidden under that cloak. That I did not has been my torture each painful day. Ever since that fateful morning – when I saw that light in your eyes – every path that I have taken – every breath that I have drawn – every blow that I have suffered is because of you. *Full of warm feelings.* And now you haunt my every moment. You are my ghost and you live four short miles away.

Do we only get one life? Is this all there will ever be? What was there for me on the other side of the membrane? What did destiny omit to tell me when I was born? Can I pick myself up from the mud and start again?

"If the little fiend had got in at the window, she probably would have strangled me."

Living on an island – Cathy and I! We want no one but ourselves! Self-sufficient – we don't want anyone else! Water comes down from the hills! Dip a bucket in the stream and light a fire! Fruit on the trees in all seasons! Pluck an orange from a tree and there's a meal! Plenty of deer to hunt – and hare! Sun at rise and sun at set finds us together! Two sets of footprints only on the beach! The ocean stretches from the bay for miles and miles!

Doesn't seem to know - sun shine on you - growing out of rock - go on at this gate - gathers the sheaves - there are no ghosts - damage their velvet clothes - all is safe - block the light - write over-top.

Oh Cathy – if you give your love to someone! If you make an eternal pledge! Then you can never love another in that way!

And if your first love turns out to be imaginary! If that person is not the other half of your soul! You will have given away – inadvertently – the best that is you!

You will be less than you could have been! A mere husk of your highest self! In exile from yourself for eternity!

She stood
on the west side.
He stood
on the east.

Damn the horses! – damn the horseshoe! I had not thought to be so delayed! The fellow is sour to be forced to repair the shoe in the dark! I flashed a few coins before his eyes and that woke him up! For these coins, my friend, I expect a most generous return! Edgar's sister plays the lady – cloaks and daggers and slashing swords! Why do you wear that silly rag across your face! Do you not see the blacksmith's wife reading your face as you hold it aside to take your drink? Your mind is as shallow as all of those puddles that soiled your fine dress on the Gimmerton road! Only about two miles, now, from the curate! Oh how I longed to see Edgar's face! Still it's best to secure the certificate – one cannot go back on that! Perhaps Edgar and Cathy together – in league against me to the end – would have dissuaded you if I had called on you at noon! The black blooms of my Heathcliff garden will soon enough see light of day! Better – much better – to plant my Heathcliff seeds in the dark!

A person spit upon by his inner-self.

All night long I lay on the landing. I could hear your father snore. I was waiting for daylight so I could be on my way. *Beseech you to explain.* Then Nelly poked me awake as I lay in exhaustion. I was amazed that I had slept, but sixty miles is a long way to walk and I was tired and the fire was warm and I slipped away. *I am led to imagine.* The old man was exhausted, too, so I didn't see him until about noon. By then I had been fed – the sight of food was a welcome one – and spit on and called bitter names by Hindley and you. *The total of my miseries.* But there was something in your eyes – Cathy – something in your eyes – something in those eyes of yours that told me that it was myself

I saw. *An unnatural dream.* Despite the spitting – despite the names – I felt that for all the rest of my days – whatever might come; whatever might go – I would dwell in you.

About a young girl who is alone in a foreign city. A pupil-teacher in a religious pensionat. Who spends her time studying foreign languages. Who is lonely – so very lonely – a soul in exile. Who yearns, at night, in her room, to be back home.

Abducting Edgar's sister.
Eloping with Cathy's sister in law.

Every day I toil and toil! Building up our fortifications! I build the walls as high as any human can! Hack and chop and lever each log into position! Take a break and admire – with Cathy – what I have done! There are trees enough on this island for massive walls! Solitary walks to gather food – the two of us! No future plans are needed – all as calm as the day we arrived! Cathy loves it here! She had grown so very weary of the outside world!

Means of livelihood - the lapwing would circle - a path hidden by drifts - no knowledge nor power - a strange presentiment - be any harm - to release the birds - a new and bitter taste - i would dwell in you - imagine seeing her eyes.

She pretended to be wounded. She dipped her wing and struggled to fly. I knew that she was trying to draw me away.
"I shall twist these thorns together. I shall make a little cage. I shall place it right above your bonny nest."
The little birds had open mouths. The mother bird made quite a noise. I fashioned my cage of thorns and set it in place.

The devil said
"I'd like to make one too."

So we've no parlours here at the Heights? Did you think that your world would never change? – or that you would transform Wuthering Heights into Thrushcross Grange? Did you see no little dark cloud in your sunny blue day? – believe there was rock beneath your feet as you walked through the bog! No – we have no parlours here! If a plain bald kitchen in not enough you can go outside in your fancy clothes and admire the flowers on the heath in the pouring rain!
A child pulling another out of a bog.
We used to go running out on the moors – hour after hour and day after day. Whatever the weather – it didn't matter. We used to dance among the

tombstones. *Locking the outer gate.* I thought the ghosts were rather silly – I told you I didn't believe in ghosts – I only believed in the here and now. I had you and you had me. Why would we want to call up the past? Why waste a moment on thought of the future? We had each other and the dairy-woman's cloak to keep out the rain. *Lived in an ancient castle.* We were out of reach of Hindley – we couldn't hear Joseph croaking of hell. Heaven was right there in the wet and the mud of the bog. So what if you lost your shoe? – we would come back and get it next day. *A look of Catherine.* We didn't talk of love or of friendship – or what the future might chance to bring. We talked of faery caves and lapwings – of melting snow and crocuses. *I did not comprehend.* And we laughed at everything that was ranged against us. We laughed at Nelly and all her warnings. We laughed at Hindley and his whip and we laughed at Joseph and his dusty old books. We laughed at those children who turned up their noses each Sunday at church.

A face with a dove's eyes.
A broken fiddle tossed on a fire.
A governess whose status is unsure.

Spice cakes in the evening. The peat fire takes the edge off the cold. Tall old tales and an occasional ballad or two. The whistling wind outside or the pouring rain.

Were you reluctant to write a novel?
Is poetry now a thing of the past?
Will you concentrate on novels from now on?

Oh, there is nothing that I can say about myself. Like everyone, I breathe the livelong day. I get up in the morning – I go to bed at night. I do my chores – whatever needs to be done. I take my walk with the dog – I think my private thoughts. 'Private' means exactly that – for me alone. I share what I have in common with the others. I never share what is particular to myself.

About the care of the children of the family. About the need to groom young ladies to catch a husband. About a young curate who comes to read the service. Whose merit she alone can appreciate. About whom, in her modesty, she has few hopes.

Tears never melted \ affection's chain \ all their anguish \ undisputed sov-
ereignty \ the night is darkening \ worth revealing \ my changeful dreams \ the
final bound \ centre both the worlds \ kill me with desire.

A dozen sheep inside a barn porch.
A box of soldiers in the sunlight on the floor.

A bitch with a swarm of squealing puppies.

Had half a mind / took our initiatory step / pictured heaven so beautifully / to run away to the moors / room in his heart / dream queer dreams / I should still continue to be / as fresh as reality / strayed to other associations / how can I tell whet ye say.

Catherine's eyes, you say? – Catherine's eyes? Yes – on Hindley and Hareton too! Now you know what a hell of my life she has made for me! She has left me to live with these creatures – the kind who would lurk in the depths of a cave! Can you imagine seeing her eyes in such monsters as these? Every day I live in this hell – the hell you imagined a faery castle – the castle to which your knight on a charger would carry you off! Be assured you are home at last – now you are seeing life as it is – all that dreaming had made you blind and I've opened your eyes!

Two young children whose lives are set at odds.

We sat together and looked in the window. All that velvet and chandeliers. Those silly children fighting and sobbing over a piddly excuse for a dog. *A half-bred bulldog.* There was no happiness in that house. No more than at Wuthering Heights. All the happiness was out on the moors – more life in the graveyard beside the old kirk. *How can I tell.* We laughed more when you lost your shoe – in the rain and the mud of that bog – than they would laugh a week in that house – than they would laugh for a month on end – than they would laugh for a year and a half at Thrushcross Grange. We looked in that window and laughed them to scorn – two silly children in fancy clothes – two shallow siblings with velvet drapes and no air to breathe. *Like a ghostly Catherine's.* I was breathing the air that you breathed – I was thinking the thoughts that you thought – when all of a sudden, that slavering beast took hold of your leg.

Each had a sheaf of paper and ink and a pen.

I dream the dream
inside the dream.
I twitch and moan
as Keeper does.

"Nelly, we's hae a crowner's 'quest enow, at ahr folks'. One on 'em 's a'most getten his finger cut off wi' hauding t' other fro' stickin' hisseln loike a cawlf. That's maister, yeah knaw, 'at 's soa up o' going tuh t' grand 'sizes. He's noan feared o' t' bench o' judges, norther Paul, nur Peter, nur John, nur Matthew, nor noan on 'em, not he! He fair likes – he langs to set his brazened face agean 'em!"

One morning – in the bay! A massive man-of-war! Sailors shouting from its decks! Cannon bristling on its sides! A message streaming from the rigging, but we cannot read the signals! Cathy wonders what they might have that we might need! A rowboat lowered into the water! A dozen sailors begin to row! Do they know we are living here? Perhaps they are only setting ashore to replenish supplies! All will be well when they are gone! As they come ashore, we retreat back into the caves!

Absorb the blows - what i meant to say - from an unknown land - a lantern and a dog - seldom sends a reply - all selfishness and distress - did a foolish thing - a desperate lapwing - pressing against a membrane - only be you and me.

Hindley was brandishing a pitchfork – an inch above my eye. I was lying on my back, looking up at the tines. In the corner of the barn – unable to move.

"You are trying to usurp my place! You are a cuckoo in the nest! I ought to poke out both your eyes, you gypsy brat!"

Best you do it now, I was thinking. The tines were dripping muck and filth. If I were in your place, I would thrust it home.

Me you above ground.
What care me you?
Me you below ground.
What care you I?

Not like this when we were courting? No I was not – sure enough! Oh the courtship – yes the courtship! It must have all come out of your books! It was you – Milady – you! – who insisted on stealing away in the dead of the night! I wanted Edgar and Cathy to watch us ride away! But you had other ideas, so I went along – for the very last time! Did you think that your brother would flog you? Or perhaps that his puny self would beat me – as your sister-in-law would say – into a pulp? Did you picture me with a dagger in my teeth – climbing up your balcony wall – come to carry you off midst the smoke and the din of a raging romantic battle – blue skies and billowing white sails – to take you and press you between the pages of one of your books?

A young boy twitching as he dreams on the hay.

All that nonsense you wrote in those books. All of that ink on all those musty pages. Why did you stop reading to me at a certain stage? You used to read to me – every word – but then you stopped. *All their beauty annihilated.* I knew you had another world that kept you in on rainy days – or you would put your books away reluctantly. All that scribbling about you and Edgar and me. *Your business here.* When I heard the word 'degrade' it was like a thunderclap. From that word my life would never be the same. I ran out into the rain. I walked all the way to Liverpool. *Like a hungry wolf.* I pried a board off a barn and crawled inside – and as I lay soaking-wet in the hay, I made a vow. That from now on I would be the one to make all the thunderclaps – that I would be the ominous portent – that I would be the darkening cloud. If there was dread it would not be for me to shrink in fear. *The hellish villain.* The vow was simple and as sharp as my hunting knife. That I would return to the neighbourhood – that I would come back after certain tasks – all to do with the further sharpening of my knife. That I would be prominent in your lives, all you who had formed a pack against me – that Hindley and the others would be the ones to be wary of me. *A soliloquy of execrations.* The only one who would not be touched would be you – Queen Cathy – you.

The young girl is taken into the house.

Torturing Edgar's sister as Cathy is torturing me.
Obsessed with talking to Cathy once again.

I am lying in the street! It is dark! – the cobblestones are wet! – it has been raining! I have no idea of time! I am between the Black Bull and the parsonage! It is a very quiet night! How long have I been lying here? – why has no one come along? Will my sisters come and look for me? – is there no one who knows I am gone? I must get home! I must get home and mix my paints! I am going to paint again! The cobblestones are wet! Torrents of rain, I assume, before dawn! I shall reach home if I have to crawl! I will work on the family portrait! The one I did before! Dead of night! – nothing stirring! – not a sound! Palette! – brushes! – paint! Just as soon as I get home! Not the steady hand of Holbein! Not the piercing eye of Reynolds! Just the eye and the hand of the painter, Branwell Brontë! – making improvements to my portrait of the Brontë Four! Lying here! – so peaceful! – let it rain!

Do her bidding - what is blame - never come true - I tug at the chain - lost his way - drops of blood - written by ellis bell - wishes piled on wishes - nothing eventful ever happened - I wod hev' ye to look out.

What do you mean we should have talked? We had no need of talk between us two! Talk is what other people do! – to figure out what they think and what they feel!
Talk is to bridge a gap! There was no gap between us two! We were on the same side of the stream!
We had silence, Cathy! Silence! A silent understanding between we two!

The defense spoke
exclusively
in the language of oranges.

Am I a man? – am I mad? – am I a devil? Be assured that to you I shall be all three! And a tiger and a venomous serpent too! You shall write of all this to your brother? – Mrs. Linton shall hear of it too? Why what a delightful threat! Let me fetch you a pen and some paper! Write whatever you please to write! I shall enjoy the idea that you tell them all that is going on! I shall make you my Edgar-proxy – and yes, my Cathy-proxy too! You shall write them a regular newssheet – with every abhorrence and every disdain! It shall stimulate my creativity – my habitual conduct shall seem tame! I shall think of countless abominations as a means of acquainting you with the madness with which Cathy is torturing me!

The cracked shell of a dream in a wind-blown nest.

What were you thinking while I was away? Through many days of agony and toil – that was the question of all my thought. Oh I was sure you would marry Edgar – yes, that was as certain as silk and champagne. *This second entrance.* But what were you thinking was the question that baffled me. An enigma – a conundrum – yes I had learned a few big words. Fancy language has always had an attraction to you. What were you thinking of the bargain? – the deal you had made to be served fine meals on silver plate? *That inhospitable hearth.* Your diamonds sparkling in the light of the chandeliers – all that I could plainly see – just as clearly as when we looked through the window that night. *Four miles distant.* But what I couldn't see was the light that had shone in your eyes. *Despair at finding nobody.* You chose yourself instead of us. How could you think that we were two? How could you take our soul and tear it like that in your hands? It has been writhing – Cathy – in torment since that day! Twisting in agony every minute from such abuse!

"A wild, wicked slip she was – but she had the bonniest eye, the sweetest smile and the lightest foot in the parish."

Sit and scribble in the clothes-press.
Sit and write in the dining room.
Clear your mind and clear the table.
Dip your pen in pots of ink.

A person calling out into a whirlwind.
Two bodies intermingling as dust.
A weight clutched fiercely in a hand.

All the books have all been written.
All the pages have been filled.
All the paper dark and musty.
All the tomes are dank and old.

Are there poems in your novel?
Would they make a better book?

Will you sprinkle some poems through the manuscript?

Are you writing in the margins?
Top and bottom, side to side?
Write as small as you can manage.
Do you think there will be room?

So let's see what you are under all this finery, Milady! I shall have my son and heir! I want a Heathcliff to rule over these houses for some time to come! A boy to drive Hindley mad with drink – should he be stubborn enough to outlive me – a boy to send Hareton out to muck in the wind and the rain! Get these petticoats over your head – forthwith – or shall tear them from your frame! You shall stand here before me as naked as any creature your god has made! Starting today your education begins! Pain, Milady, pain! – pain without tears – the worst kind of pain! You shall find out what it can be to live in this world!

A human being passing through a great oak door.

Well, Cathy, this is the end of it – I can tolerate no more! I will see you though I be forced to break down the door! *I had sought shelter.* Though Edgar sic the dogs against me I will force my way into your presence! If you are dying, I shall die too! If you are living, we shall live together! It is either myself or Edgar – chandeliers or humble porridge – you cannot have both! *A woman's voice.* I want an end to all of this misery – misery for you and misery for me! I had rather be a ghost than draw my breath in such searing pain, day after day! *Must wait on yourself.* Is it life or is it death? – you must decide!

Chapter 14

Cathy 7

The page unlined and blank. Only seven by nine, with stiff pasteboard covers, but enough of a world to me. All I am and all I imagine – all I have been and all I will be. I only sit here for a moment before I dip my pen in the ink and start to write.

A tale whose words have failed to please.

Waiting for something – waiting for something. What am I waiting for? A sense that something has been in the garden for days and days. *The consequence was.* A white dress. Oh why a white dress? What did whiteness used to mean? Dresses the envy of every pert lass in the neighbourhood. *So warm and pleasant.* I sit here at the open window and wonder why I cannot feel the breeze. It ruffles the curtains but it does not make an impression on my hand. It has turned a number of pages of this book. *Locking the doors.* One of Edgar's unreadable books, left here on the windowsill. If I had the strength I would fling it down into this bog. *Set them wide open.* Oh, why would I want to read a book? The book of me has been indecipherable. I can see no meaning at all. Every word that I have written is a hieroglyph. *To gaze beyond.* All my loves have gone along on their merry way.

To be

A child from an unknown land.
A clutch of little skeletons in a nest.
A whip lying on a country road.

a name chiselled into

Ever think of your long-dead mother?
Your two elder sisters who departed this earth?
Are all these people still alive, in a sense, to you?

a block of stone.

A girl whose sister tells her she cannot spell.
Pewter dishes, silver jugs and rows of tankards.
A gate with an unremovable chain.

The chapel bells are ringing, Nelly. The water is sounding in the brook. Where does the water come from, Nelly?
Two persons exchanging words in an unknown tongue.
Are children wading, can you see? What is that house beyond the hill with the strangest name? The children from that house used to wade and laugh for hours in the stream. *Break the seal.* A letter is placed in my hand. Who would send a missive to me? Don't they know that I am no longer receiving mail? *Gleam of recollection.* Bad news is a flying steed, Nelly; good news is a wounded mule. *Struggle to arrange her ideas.* Oh, I cannot bear to read it. Who would sue for a boon from me? Is it written in hieroglyphics? I find I cannot recognize the name.

Does life have paths that we must follow? Do we never get a choice? I was the one who was the exception! I was the one who would make his mark! If we leave the path is there nothing but a bog?

"That minx, Catherine Linton or Earnshaw, or however she was called – she must have been a changeling – wicked little soul!"

I find myself at the window! The night is cold and wet! It is my room at Wuthering Heights! There has been no light in this room since I was a girl! I used to light a candle! I used to sit in my bed! – draw the panels so no one could see me! I would take a pen and a bottle of ink and write my story in the margins of the dusty old books!

A station exposed - reached the loftiest heights - what do you gather - lived
in their minds - the gleaner who scours - no one living or dead - would never
fight - kidnaped by pirates - perused them many times - my story is mine.

Nelly Dean does not know the story! Nor does that man who seized my wrist! I have come to you to tell me what you know!
Whatever I have done to please you! What I have done to break your heart! That is a very small part of the story that must be told!
Some day we'll sit by the fire! A blaze of peat as we sit on the rocks! And

we will laugh about the things that made us cry!

She pushed
towards the east.
He pushed
towards the west.

A creature clasps me in his arms! He puts his cheek against my cheek! He kisses me but he dare not look me in the face! *Two people cheek to cheek with their lips sewn shut.* Who is this who holds me, Nelly? I have no idea who this could be at all! I clasp his hair and turn his face and look deep into his eyes! *Consider a stranger.* Oh it is Heathcliff, my childhood companion! I had forgotten that you were alive! Did you bring the old dairy-woman's cloak? It always rains and storms whenever we go outside! *At her side.* But you have not come here for my comfort! You cannot fool me with tears in your eyes! You have come here searching for jewels in a darkened mine! But you have pulled down the emperor's columns! You have cracked the very foundations! *Grasped in his arms.* Did you not like the crimson cushions? See no light in the chandeliers? We could have all sat by the fire and sipped our tea! *Nor loosed his hold.* Face to face with the one who betrayed me! Are we face to face in heaven? – are we are face to face in hell? *Downright agony.* You speak but I cannot hear you! It is only my voice that I hear! I can only hear my voice – I cannot hear you!

But the extraordinary man is a married man. It is a love that can never be. She suffers much – she suffers greatly. Who could describe the relentless agony? She feels condemned to spend the rest of her life alone.

Sitting by the open window.
No one ever comes to call.

I find myself at the window! There is a candle glowing inside! I rap gently on the window! I must tell my soul I am here! Only Heathcliff would sleep in this room! I gently knock to bring him awake! A hole is broken in the glass! I reach out towards my soul! A hand reaches out and clutches! It rubs my wrist on the jagged shard! Why would my Heathcliff do this to me? My blood runs down the pane and I shrink from his touch! Oh Heathcliff – let me in! I have been out here in the cold for twenty years!

Fire at its hottest - I say not a thing - hiding with cathy - those who re-mained behind - into someone else - a mixed fairy-tale - to bring the breezes - dream of a thunderclap - a soul in exile - seeing life as it is.

I thought of you, Heathcliff, as the rock on which my entire world was founded! I took it for granted that it would always – always – bear me up! Through wind and rain it was the ground on which I stood!

You took that rock away! There was no centre to my earth! My life with Edgar had no rock on which I stood!

Oh why did you leave me, Heathcliff? We were lapwings caught in the storm! I was trying to bring you in from the wind and the rain!

"You may make
a menacing monster
to terrorize the earth."

Broken my heart! – Yes, broken my heart! That is what you and Edgar have done!

Shallow people of petty concerns at the door of the kirk.

And now you come to ask for pity? – pity for you but not for me? You who have broken my every dream! You and Edgar are a chorus of selfishness! For the two of you I can have no pity at all! *Oh my life.* Have you brought your woven basket! What is the harvest you would glean? *Broken my heart.* You trampled all my magnanimity in the mud of your own concerns! You fed on loaves of love while my meal was a crumb or two! *You have killed me.* You will go on to love many others! You will be here when I am gone! You will have children – a nest full of children! They will show you their petty toys – standing in front of the faded vision you will have of me! You will walk by my grave in the churchyard – many years after I turn to dust – sorry to think that I am somewhere waiting for you! *You have thriven on it.* I heard the sound of the brook this morning, Heathcliff! I have drowned in its waters while you are still perfectly dry!

A hand crushing a rotten hazel-nut.
A young girl dressed in velvet and in furs.
A terrified child held over a bannister.

Well, we live very simply here. There are five of us in the house. Father, Branwell, Charlotte, Anne and myself. Tabby is our servant, but is getting old. We do as much around here as needs be done.

Your father, your sisters, your brother?
Are these people real to you?
Does real, to a writer, mean something you've written about?

Cauterize myself with a poker? – well, I was bitten by a dog. There is nothing more to tell. Yes, I suppose I would have died. Yes, the pain was quite intense, but it simply seemed, at the time, the thing to do.

About the humiliating grind of life as a governess. About the silly, vacuous children of the idle rich. About the crude and inane dining-room conversations. About being worked by the mistress like a plough horse. And of having never a moment to oneself.

Spirit's icy pride \ thy soul was pure \ to call back night \ star followed star \ thought followed thought \ proves us one \ his fierce beams \ things which cannot be \ the ear begins to hear \ vanished with the morn.

A servant with a lantern and a dog.
A girl with a face the size of a penny.
Lines in dark ink on a white page.

Unable to remove the chain / sought a separate nook / that ever ransacked a bible / burning their eyes out / to make a fiend of a saint / dreams that have stayed with me / the universe would turn / a gush of child's sensations / entirely her former self / my dreams appal me.

I kiss him! I kiss my betrayer! I kiss him again and again and again!
Two jailers locking each other in adjacent cells.
You speak but I do not hear you! I can only hear my own words! *Wretched to lose her.* If you see death in my face, my Heathcliff, it is you who have put it there! But don't think that you have been spared your just desserts! *Strange and fearful picture.* I shall never be at peace, my Heathcliff, if you are not at peace! It has been so in life, my Heathcliff – every welt on your back has left a scar on me! *Branded in my memory.* It will be so while I am dead! If you are miserable, I will be miserable! I will feel it under the ground! I will feel every pain that you inflict on others – I will feel every pain that is ever inflicted on you! I have had agonies untold while I have been queen of the neighbourhood! Unknown to you I have suffered your every mood! *Shall not be at peace.* So why have you stifled your every promise? You are a prince in a Heathcliff disguise! Love is not love which does not bring peace! You have murdered our shared soul! *Never to be parted.* The Heathcliff that I have known is not the Heathcliff that you have known! You have missed out on the best that is buried in you! Oh do not look at me with those eyes! The prison that I have been living in is you!

She closed her eyes and thought for a moment.

I awake with my
hand in the water.
The tiny tadpoles
dance and dart.

"And yon bonny lad Heathcliff, yah mind, he's a rare 'un. He can girn a laugh as well 's onybody at a raight divil's jest. Does he niver say nowt of his fine living amang us, when he goes to t' Grange?"

I find myself at the window! I can hear the voice of my Heathcliff! I can hear the voice of my soul! He is crying out for me to come inside! I press myself against the window! The blood runs down my arm! I cannot see my Heathcliff! Can he hear my voice in turn? Why can we not be reunited? I cannot see through the glass! It is a mirror – not a window! Why is my face the only face that I can see?

Softened every insult - sitting on the throne - alive, in a sense - putting them in a novel - elements that are intolerable - i am an angel - a major mistake - surrounded by snarling dogs - faintly hear a heartbeat - each write a novel.

I made a nest out of whatever I could find! Out of twigs and wisps of hay! Out of mud and tufts of grass!

I had very little choice! Whatever happened to be floating down the stream! I lined it with the feathers of other birds!

I made a shelter for us both! You ran out in the wind and the storm! We couldn't spend the rest of our lives on the heath!

Me you eye eye.
What care me you?
Me you know know.
What care you I?

So what to do about it all? – what to do about it all? We must decide what to do for eternity!

Two children holding hands at a fork of a path.

If you love me – never leave me! That is the test and the only test! I lay this curse upon you, Heathcliff! I lay a greater curse upon myself! A curse that will last for all of time! *Looking absolutely desperate.* So long as you are not free, I shall not be free! – so long as you are in prison, I shall be there to share your cell! *Locked in an embrace.* Oh I am dying Heathcliff, dying, but whatever is promised to others will not be for me! I abjure whatever glorious world is waiting for me to arrive! You are me and I am you – I am your soul and you are my soul! *Gathered her to him.* We shall be one, in life and in death, for better or for worse! We shall neither be in this world nor in my grave! Shall we be wading in the beck? Shall we be running on the moors? Shall we be peaking in at windows to see what's inside? We shall soon see! – we shall soon see! – we shall soon see! *He would not understand.* If you destroy me, I must destroy you! If I redeem you, you must redeem me! I shall be waiting – always waiting – on the other side of the glass! On the other side of the membrane! Waiting under the nab! Waiting for you to come along with me!

She falls in love with scented dresses and chandeliers.

Deserted by Heathcliff and Edgar.
Knowing that I am dying alone.

I sit and write these letters! He seldom sends a reply! Perhaps I should promise to cease if he'll deign to answer just one! It is months now since he has spared me even one word! I wonder whether he gets to read them? Surely his wife would not be so bold! The extremes of the year are upon us! I wonder whether he minds the cold! Be sure to dress warmly when stepping outside! It can be cold, as you know, in Belgium! These sudden chills can take a person by surprise! You'll be pleased to know that I keep myself up on my French! I memorize at least a page a day! Oh some days that is impossible, though I assure you that I try! It's just that some days there are distractions! Some days our lives are pulled each way! But then things settle down and the waves subside! Please send me just one letter! Please say that your life has turned out well! I want nothing for myself! I only want to hear well of you! You might mention your wife and children! I would hope that they all are well! It is your mind that I found so inspiring! It seems we sat and talked for hours! Of course I have my sisters! But otherwise, there is little here of a level of discourse in which one can exercise one's own best thoughts! Talk here is of the weather, or of slips and pillowcases, or of the darning of Branwell's socks! I want only a few words of comfort! Things have gone badly for me of late! There are elements that are intolerable in all our lives! I only want to imagine a friend who thinks well of me! I only want to be able to think of you as a friend! I shall mail this on the morrow, weather come or weather go! Just one word is all I ask of you! Perhaps you would prefer that this letter from me should be the last?

Both sides of the window - the answers are stored - grovel in such pain - i was a ghost - pits beside the pathway - piece of broken glass - never been as close - one who brings the news - on opposite sides of the globe - how to read your markers.

We must make haste, my Heathliff! Who can know whether this moment will last? What is the meaning of that sob I hear in your voice?
What of my daughter? What of Edgar? What of the world I left behind?
Twenty years have gone by in a moment! The generations go by in a flash! Tell me what has transpired while I've been hovering over my grave!

"Solomon used a knife,"
said the clerk

of the court.

I spring towards my Heathcliff! We are locked in an embrace! I will never let you go while we are alive! I shall cling to you when I am in the grave!
Three elements which refuse to meld into one.
But what is this? – what is this? Your lips are moving though I cannot hear your voice! You turn your face away from me! You look towards the door! *Clasp his neck.* Ellen is pointing and waving frantically for you to go! I put my hand upon your neck and draw you to me! I put my cheek upon your cheek and cling to you! *If I've done wrong.* We cling with our faces hidden! We are washed by a million tears! *Bring her cheek to his.* After what seems an eternity, you face me! You pull yourself from my arms and speak to me! *I'm dying for it.* You must not go – you shall not go! You and Edgar must shake hands! You must be brothers! – you must sip your tea and talk! *You left me too.* You whisper words I cannot hear! You are Heathcliff – I know you are Heathcliff! *I forgive you.* Edgar enters into the room! I feel my strength receding! You take me in your arms! – you pass me over to Edgar! – my head bounces against his arm! *Forgive me.* Now you leave me! – Heathcliff! – you leave me! How terrible to have to die alone!

"She was much too fond of Heathcliff. The greatest punishment we could invent for her was to keep her separate from him; yet she got chided more than any of us on his account."

Marry the fairest in the country.
Take her home to your estate.
First lady of the district.
Idle chatter over tea.

A girl who is teaching an unruly child.
Three people at a table sipping tea.
A young prince begging on the streets.

There are clouds above the hillside.
Cold winds rattle at the door.
Have the servant fix the fire.
Turn the pages of your book.

All these people – dead and alive?
Ever think of putting them in a novel?
Ever wonder what such a book would be?

What is wrong with the faery princess?
What does 'ever-after' mean?

What does she want that you cannot give her?
Angels wonder what she needs.

And now you – Edgar – are leaving me too. Can one so easily be forgotten? The first lass of the neighbourhood?
Living books and dying people telling tales.
Fine dresses each Sunday at church – a coach and two with gleaming harness – nodding to the servants as we pass. Did it ever occur that we were nodding to me? *The life-less looking form.* All those times we sat by the window and sipped our tea – all the sunlight and all the shadows all passing away. *Restore her to sensation.* Nelly is telling you to forsake me – I am hearing her every word. She is telling you that I am better when she knows quite well that I shall die. *The half-opened door.* Nelly – the teller of tales. Go at sunrise to the brook, Nelly, which flows down from high in the hills. The headwaters will send you the fiercest of all the tales you might live to tell. Come the morrow, every ear will be turned to you. *Delivered the house.* And Edgar – beloved Edgar – who locks himself in his reading room. No doubt your shelf of books is calling – books and books in rows and rows – Catherine Linton is the name on every spine. Tell me Edgar – tell me Edgar – I have always meant to ask. Is there a book of Catherine Earnshaw on your shelf? If so, have you ever cut the leaves?

Chapter 15

Heathcliff 7

Keeper is a good old dog! Keeper is a good old dog! – yes he is! Keeper comes out with me in all kinds of weather – weather good or weather bad. He never gives his Emily any problems. He lies down here at my feet and lets me write. Though Keeper sometimes wants a little too much attention – yes you do! If I don't rub you on the head every once in a while – though I am deep in another world – my Keeper groans!

A little boy locked out in the cold and the rain.

Waiting in the garden. Cathy is somewhere in the house. She is a prisoner and Edgar is clutching the key. *Expressed no recognition.* Edgar and his gang are gone to church to simper and to pray. I am lurking here in the garden awaiting my cue. *It wants an answer.* Best he pray for forgiveness for all the harm he has done. Better he stay there the rest of the day on his knees. If he were here, I would gladly tear him limb from limb from limb – I would enjoy the act of feeding him to his dogs. *Had not gathered its import.* He is a monster and I am a lamb. Cathy has led me to his altar. Together they have drained the blood from my veins. *Questioning eagerness.* Oh where is a rock to smash these windows? Where is Nelly to open the door as she said she would do?

To be able

Writing materials strewn across a lawn.
An elderly man stopping to wind a clock.
A thousand hammers beating inside a skull.

to talk to people

Did you set the trap for the lapwings?
Lose your shoe in the mud of the bog?
Watch yourself sip champagne neath the chandelier?

after one dies.

Birthday papers sealed for a future time.
A fine summer morning at the beginning of harvest.
Purple heather, fern and bilberry leaves.

I am keyed-up like a wolf about to spring!
Two people in an embrace of life and death.
A stride and I have clasped you in my arms! Five long minutes we hold each other! Many kisses we both bestow! *Neither spoke.* I lean back and look at your face and I see death at work inside! *Downright agony.* Oh do not try to speak, my love! We never used to talk – remember how little we used to say? We would spend hours on the moors without a word! *Had stricken him.* I fight down the urge to blame you – what is blame at a moment like this? When I ask how I can bear it, I bite my tongue! *There was no prospect.* Let us hold each other forever without a word!

All the past came back to haunt him. Thoughts tormented his fevered brain. The most galling thoughts ever known to the mind of man. So he lay there on the ground – dust and dung on the cobblestones. Far below the lofty towers where the answers are stored.

"My companion found it necessary to warn me frequently to steer to the right or left, when I imagined I was following, correctly, the windings of the road."

I find myself at the window! I fling the fool aside! How dare you come into this room! What possessed you to enter here? I will tear out your throat if you intrude in this way again! What did you see here? What have you heard? What did you say to call up such a vision? What are the words you spoke to her? Oh, get out of my way and let me see her once more!

Life unknown to you - soared above your heads - what do you trample - suffering indignities - light my future sky - they all grew older - watch every-thing they do - wastes away and dies - a story to make - no one will ever know.

When two people love each other such as we two, there are forces that constantly threaten to break them apart! Hindley and Edgar – heaven and hell – but never me! Only one force could break the bond between you and me!
There were people at Wuthering Heights! There were people at Thrush-

cross Grange! The only place for us was as far away from others as we could be!

We were best when we were alone! Out on the moors! Even the lapwings were a distraction – don't you see?

To this day
the stone
in the path
has never moved.

You start to speak but I shake my head! I want to hear none of these terrible words! Whatever wisdom you think you have learned, I don't want to hear now!

Two waifs caught in a shower of babbling words.

No – I will not listen to you Cathy! I will hear not a word that you have to say! *Don't torture me.* I have heard it all before – many times and in many words! It is a false-Cathy who has been talking – it is not the Cathy I know! I lost my Cathy at the window – when that dog seized your ankle that day at Thrushcross Grange! From that moment I heard not one pure word from you! *Mad as yourself.* Tie your cravat! – polish your grammar! – be sure to trim those dreadful nails! You never talked like this when we used to run on the moors!

But the extraordinary man is a married man. It is a love that can never be. She suffers much – she suffers greatly. Who could describe the relentless agony? She feels condemned to spend the rest of her life alone.

Waiting in the garden for a signal.
Forcing my way into Cathy's room.

I find myself at the window! I call out to my living soul! So you have come at last, Cathy! I have waited twenty years! It has been twenty years of agony! Twenty years without my soul! Come to the window! Come to the window! Oh I know you have been close by! You have appeared to the little shepherd! Other children have seen you as well! I cannot see you! – I cannot see you! Why appear to others and never appear to me!

Pressed our hands together - think of cheer-fuller things - stalking with heathcliff - when they were made - an exile and an outcast - attempts to calm - a range of gaunt thorns - away from prying eyes - an occasional ballad - made you blind.

We were walking along the road. He was getting short of breath. He had told me that the journey was sixty miles.

"I am in need of a son and heir. You shall never rue the day. I have no one to inherit when I die."

His walk was no more than a shuffle. I didn't believe a word he said. He sat down on a stone and clutched his chest.

The devil smiled
and said
"I'll make a cuckoo."

I attempt to rise but you seize my hair and pull me down! Don't torture me I say and wrench my hair from out of your grasp and grind my teeth! *A bulldog with an ankle in its teeth.* My eyes melt into yours and your eyes melt into mine! *Possessed with a devil.* We have always been one person – Oh Cathy, how could you break us apart? *Branded in your memory.* How could you do such a thing to the one that was me and you? *Infernal selfishness.* I cannot hear a word you say! – I will not hear a word you say! I did not come here to listen or to talk! *Writhe in the torments of hell.* There is no future for us now! – only a moment to speak of the past! – the past that you tainted as one would poison the purest stream!

Two ghosts who are looking for a home.
A servant telling a story to a guest.
A girl who hails a boat in the Thames.

Howarth is seldom visited by those who might consider themselves to be outsiders. However, it is safe, no doubt, to say that all that is human takes place here – and on the moors.

Did you hear that life would degrade you?
Howl all night in the pouring rain?
Tear the feathers from the pillow with your teeth?

Has Charlotte been telling you of events, here, at the parsonage? She has a tendency to dramatize. Not everything that we do is worth talking about.

About a girl in a less than satisfying position. Who sets her chin and fixes her mind. Who schools herself to endure the petty slights. To keep her disapproval under wraps. Whose goodness is rewarded in the end.

All the woe creation knows \ a thousand strains of music \ held backward \ the waves efface \ one sweet influence \ dreadful is the check \ the wolf's death howl \ comes every night to me \ loved her all the night \ more glory and more grief.

A cheerful fire and smoking coffee.
A housekeeper who writes an occasional poem.
A canine mother who emits a guttural snarl.

Knocked vainly for admittance / a scamper on the moors / wishing we were all there safe together / a prince in disguise / it can't be helped / did not seem to be my home / the foliage in the woods / deny you hereafter admission / held the casement ajar / you must wait on yourself.

I cannot let you see my face! I turn my face away! *Eyes blinded by the glare of unwept tears.* I stand and look down at the fireplace! I choke back anger! – I choke back tears! *Cruel and false.* I will not listen to what you are saying – I will not turn and look in your eyes! *Betray your own heart.* You Cathy! – You! You are the only one on earth who could ever have done me harm – and you have done so! You are the only person in the world before whom I have stood completely unarmed! *No one word of comfort.* Yours is the deepest of all the knives – the only knife which has left a mark beyond the skin! *Have killed yourself.* My face is wet with my emotions! Since the day you disappeared, I have never been one for tears! From this day I shall never cry again!

A young girl appeared at a window.

I arise and look
around me.
The air is
fresh and clean and pure.

"This is t' way on 't: – up at sun-down: dice, brandy, cloised shutters, und can'le-light till next day at noon: then, t'fooil gangs banning und raving to his cham'er, makking dacent fowks dig thur fingers i' thur lugs fur varry shame; un' the knave, why he can caint his brass, un' ate, un' sleep, un' off to his neigh-bour's to gossip wi' t' wife."

I find myself at the window! I feel your breath upon my cheek! I see your blood run down the pane! I shall thrash the clod who has hurt you! Tear out his throat and drink his blood! Oh, but Cathy – why have you come here? Why are you here after twenty long years? And why can I not see you with these eyes? Why can I not see my Cathy? Why can we not be reunited? I cannot see through the glass! It has the attributes of a mirror! Why is my face the only face that I can see?

In like predicament - hostile dog or hungry rat - people of petty concerns - what such a book would be - things have gone badly - all live in peace - think strange thoughts - a boy without a penny - a breath upon my cheek - good old dog.

I was lying in a rowboat. A large man was plying the oars. The sun was beating down and the seagulls flew.

"Quite a feat to rescue you, my lad. If they want you, they'll pay quite handsomely. If not, you'll be a rat in the Liverpool slums."

A voice called out in a foreign tongue. He pushed me down against the wood. He covered me with a blanket from head to foot.

Me you found lost.
What care me you?
Me you lost found.
What care you I?

I hear a movement and I turn towards you! You are springing into my arms!

A membrane slowly forming an impenetrable seal.

I carry you to the sofa and you sprawl across my lap! Oh how can I bear to look at your dying face? *They'll blight you.* Oh do not kiss me – or hug me – or hold me – it is only breaking my heart! *What right had you.* It will do no good in this world! *Misery and degradation.* We had life right here in our hands and you threw it away!

The young boy looks through the window at the young girl.

Trying to remain silent while I hold my Cathy.
Exchanging with Cathy these hated words.

My mind has a natural bent for noble instruction. I long to dedicate myself to the edification of those of my sex who are almost the equal of my own age. I do not have the constitution which the post of governess requires – not that of a horse, as Charlotte says, no, nor that of a galley-slave – but I do have abundant desire that I should do some good in this world, as much as my limited talents will allow me to do. How to serve? – how to serve? – how best for me to serve? Well Charlotte's idea – of course – yes, Charlotte's idea! Take pen and paper and write a book – a book of exemplary edification. A novel – as Charlotte suggests – one that will be of service to countless young ladies for whom such guidance is sorely in need – like these girls I have tried so hard to win at Thorp Green. Yes – the three of us writing novels – we must coax Emily to write one too. The three of us at the table – each of us dipping our pens in the ink – each of us setting down scenes of the actual life on the page. I cannot wait to return to the parsonage – at home in the dining room once again – our pen-nibs scratching as the ink flows onto the page.

Try to look out - steer to the right or the left - if I have my way - people were so cold - far from human - wards of the church - gone the images - one more bairn - something was pulling me - rules for entrance.

When two people love each other, they can walk out onto the air! They can walk out over a canyon or a bog! And always – always – always – a bridge will form at every step – a bridge will constantly form and re-form under their feet!

And they can see vistas far and wide! Vistas that no one else can see – the joy so high above and the pain below! And always they will be safe as long as the two are holding hands!

But if one should withdraw a hand – even if meant for a moment or two – the bridge will disappear and both will tumble down! Where is your hand, Cathy? – where is your hand? – I am holding mine out to you! I beg you – I implore you – reach out to me!

"In this case,
not even Solomon
could proceed."

We hug each other fiercely! I cannot bear to look in your face!
A guttered candle in a sliver of moonlight in a darkened room.
Oh how smug you are in your madness! *God or Satan could inflict.* You shall go to your just reward – in Ellen's heaven or in Joseph's hell – and leave me all alone on this earth with but half a soul! *What kind of living.* Wading through ashes every day! – the burnt-out ruins of all my hopes! Not a shred of colour by day! – not a sliver of moon or stars to relieve my night! *Soul in the grave.* The sound of Edgar on the stairway! Ellen cries that I should go! *Love my murderer.* Let him shoot me if he so wishes, only let me die with my Cathy in my arms!

"Her pretended insolence, which he thought real, had more power over Heathcliff than his kindness; how the boy would do her bidding in anything."

Man and boy walk on the roadway.
Boy and man.
Man and boy.
One is talking and one is listening as they walk.

Flames licking round a red-hot key.
Veins filled with boiling, dancing blood.
The child of a Chinese prince or an Indian queen.

Boy and girl run through the heather.

Girl and boy.
Boy and girl.
One is singing and one is silent as they run.

Do you appear on both sides of the window?
Try to look out and try to look in?
Has your soul been torn in two for twenty years?

Bird and chicks on the moorland.
Chicks and bird.
Bird and chicks.
One is flying and some are chirping as they wait.

I howl like an animal! I bash my head against a tree! I am desolate! – desolate! – desolate!

A servant coming in the dark to bear the news.

Oh Cathy! – oh my Cathy! You have died inside my being – a lightning strike inside my soul! You have died and you have left me here alive! *In torment.* My life stretches out before me as one long aching echo of this moment when your heart has ceased to beat! I curse the blood that animates my veins! *Inward agony.* No – I shall not let you go! I bring this curse upon you, Cathy! May you never leave this earth! Many you never reach heaven nor hell! *May you not rest.* May you be like the ghosts you conjured when you were dancing in the churchyard! I call on you as you once called on all of those slumbering souls! You had no pity on them and I shall have no pity on you! *In this abyss.* I won't be dancing as you have done – I shall be stomping on your grave! – my face will haunt you as you try to close your eyes! May you never rest until I am a ghost with you! *Cannot find you.* Nelly comes out from the house! She is coming, as she thinks, to bear the news! She fancies herself as the source of all the wisdom there is in the world, but Nelly has never had any conception of Cathy and me! *Without my soul.* There is nothing that Nelly can say that I care to know!

Chapter 16

Emily 2

Keeper! – my soul-mate, Keeper! Hard to believe I got so cross at you that day! Were you as surprised as Charlotte and Anne? Should I flatter myself and say that it wasn't me? Well here we are together – no matter what has come between us – you and me.

A writer about characters who are far from human.

Almost done – just a few more pages – I have an idea for a finishing touch. Wrap it round with a colourful ribbon and tie it snug with a great big bow. What a surprise for whoever peeks in to see what is inside.

To be

A boy walking home covered in mud.
A woman threatened with swallowing a carving knife.
A dead woman who wonders about her daughter.

a sister

Have you shown this novel to your sisters?
To your father or your brother at all?
Would it matter to you what anyone might say?

sitting and writing at a table.

A newspaper article about a ship trapped in the ice.
A pail of porridge for the dogs.
A row of loose stones fashioned into a wall.

Do publishers correct an author's spelling? Are they free to change the words?

A novel of natures relentless and implacable.

Charlotte says we shall sign a contract which will determine what is what. Well, I, for one, will peruse such a contract quite carefully.

And then, one night, he sobered up for just a moment. And he took his paints and brushes. And he mixed himself a wash. And he put the family portrait on the easel. And he painted himself out of the Brontë Four.

"I desired Mrs. Dean, when she brought in supper, to sit down while I ate it; hoping sincerely she would prove a regular gossip, and either rouse me to animation or lull me to sleep by her talk."

What will Charlotte have to say when she reads this?

Since before time began - years of agony - left out on the moors - escaping and running loose - coaxing the fire - the sole support - go on at this gate - bone-chilling walk - a sheaf of blank pages - the clock ticks loudly.

We must talk, Heathcliff – talk – as we have never done before! All of our differences were simply for lack of speaking out loud! Tell me all about your life for these lost twenty years!

*Little skeletons
in a nest.*

Another novel? Perhaps – I do have a few ideas.

A novel hewn in a wild workshop with simple tools.

I can't say I've been surprised by what I have written here. That others might well be surprised is nothing to me. What I have written, I have written – take it or leave it as you please. I would write differently if I were a different me.

Each night she sat at the table. One sister on her right and one on her left. Every so often, she would stop and think for a moment. The clock was the only sound in the silent room. Then she would dip her pen in the ink and continue to write.

Sitting at the table and writing.

Charlotte on my left and Anne on my right.

What will Anne have to say when she reads this?

*Wiped his hand - roof will fall - an ancient story - a touch of madness -
empty out the slops - listening and thinking - you have ruined everything - what
is a novel - breathe the livelong day - one lone high-flying hawk.*

I shall starve myself to death, Cathy, as you did so long ago! I should have
done it then! You were right and I was wrong to live so long!

*Gone the thoughts
they chirped in spring.*

We move our pens across the paper. Each one dipping into the inkwell as
each has need. Once in a while, a pause.
A novel which is a granite block on a solitary moor.
Interesting from Charlotte – about a madwoman in an attic. I'll be the
madwoman in my novels, I laugh and say.

*A young boy hiding in a barn.
A rat in the gutters of Liverpool.
Drops of blood on a piece of broken glass.*

I've never cared for life away from the parsonage. It is hard to say what
it is. I suppose I tend to think of this as my home. Of course, we do not own
the parsonage. We are all of us wards of the church. In effect, we Brontës are
temporary here.

Do you see yourself as different from other people?
Is this novel about you or about everyone but you?
About the life you have lived or the life you have failed to live?

Well, that is enough for now. I am not the chatty kind. Our day begins at
sunrise and chores are done by nine o'clock. All of our life is composed of
family routine. That is all I have to say of the enterprise. Not worth the breath
to tell. Nothing happens here that I would call momentous. If anything happens, Charlotte or Anne will let you know.

She would sit for hours in the evening. Her two sisters sat one on either
side. A moment's thought, from time to time, as to what would happen next.
A glance, perhaps, at the quietly-ticking clock. Then she would dip her pen in
the ink and write again.

*Worlds of light \ my anchor of desire \ as they were life \ endless bliss
through endless years \ endure the woe \ the world without \ the leveret's cry \
true to all \ intense the agony \ all the flowers are praying.*

Oatcakes, legs of beef, mutton and ham.
A hand stirring tadpoles in a cold stream.
A dairy-woman's cloak on a peg.

Perpetual isolation / writing scratched on the paint / the lightest foot in the parish / could not comprehend / I've marked every day / the colour of my mind / the eternal rocks beneath / convince you of the contrary / wish you would speak rationally.

Ink and paper – ink and paper. That is as far as resemblance goes. Three of us sitting at the table – sharing paper, pens and ink. Writing of three different kingdoms in separate worlds. Where is the reader with the thread to bind these words?

Wrapping paper – cost of postage. Addresses of publishers – a question of names.
A novel which is moorish, wild and knotty as a root of heath.
Interesting from Anne – about a warning to young females contemplating matrimony. No warnings in my novels, I say. I'll pull open every gate along the way.

She dipped the pen in the ink and started to write.

I climb the stile behind the parsonage.
Clouds are gathering far above.
I walk into this room
and I sit in this chair.

"I' course, he tells Dame Catherine how her fathur's goold runs into his pocket, and her fathur's son gallops down t' broad road, while he flees afore to oppen t' pikes!"

What will a publisher have to say when he reads this?

A story to enact - bread and drink - broken my every dream - you cannot give her - interesting thoughts today - the one who gives the cue - there was a membrane - a law-abiding citizen - without a significant function - weather good and weather bad.

Meet me on the heath, my darling! Meet me on the moors! Oh Heathcliff – we have never been as close as we are soon to be!

Gone the images

of their dreams.

Choosing names to suit ourselves – Currer, Ellis and Acton Bell. Insisting that never, never – never – must Charlotte ever reveal our secret to any publisher or reviewer or reader – no, not even to her friends.
An author with a suspicious nom de plume.
I shall always be Emily Brontë. This novel shall always have been written by Ellis Bell.

Will the children ever again run free on the moors?

Sitting at the table and writing.
A few more words and the task will be done.

What will a reviewer have to say when he reads this?

Try to look in - fling the fool aside - eyes evincing scorn - i didn't recognize my voice - finishing touch - temporary here - names to suit - as slate or as granite - whether forgiveness is an issue - rules for expulsion.

I shall meet you on the heath, my darling! I shall meet you on the moors! Oh Cathy – we will soon be closer than we were ever able to be!

*The only music
in their skulls
is the moorland breeze.*

Nelly Dean told a tale; Mr. Lockwood told one too. Mr. Lockwood told his tale to me and now I tell my tale to you.
A writer with a strange tale to tell.
How would either of us now know what is true?

"The little souls were comforting each other with better thoughts than I could have hit on; no parson in the world ever pictured heaven so beautifully as they did, in their innocent talk, and while I sobbed and listened, I could not help wishing we were all there safe together."

*A king in an ancient kingdom.
A queen in a foreign land.
Miles and years beyond each other.
Sitting on their royal thrones.*

*A table with paper, pens and ink.
Three graves on the edge of a cemetery.*

Pine-cones tapping against a window.

Sad the news that came on the waves.
Sad the news that came on the wind.
The little prince is not returning.
He will not be home again.

What will this novel do for its author?
What will it do for everyone else?
Have you asked yourself just what does a novel do?

The child-size throne is sitting empty.
On the floor some royal toys.
Where has gone the royal princeling?
What the life in what the land?

Cathy wrote a novel; Heathcliff wrote one too. Cathy's was voluminous; Heathcliff barely wrote a word.

Heathcliff and a woman yonder, under t' nab.

They combined them in two volumes. They are meeting on the heath to write the third.

Three Books

Emily Brontë: More Myself Than I – a novel
Every evening, flanked by her two creative sisters, Charlotte and Anne, Emily Brontë sits down at the dining-room table in the Haworth parsonage and writes. As she does so, her imagination compresses and transforms the information of the life-experience that surrounds her – in the parsonage and out on the moors – into the diamond-hard imagery of her novel, *Wuthering Heights*.

The Making of Emily Brontë: More Myself Than I – a reflective journal
This journal records the author's reflections on the process of the crafting of the novel as it evolved through the stages of planning, writing, editing and polishing. It constitutes an effort to be as conscious as possible of the process whereby the single idea that suggested the topic of the novel was expanded into a complex work of art. Topics range from the nuts and bolts of novel-building to the nature of the novel as an art-form.

Planning Emily Brontë: More Myself Than I – a planning notebook
During the writing of the novel, the author kept a hand-written notebook which records the day-by-day development of the novel as it found its shape and style. The notebook – now in print form – reveals how a vast cluster of thoughts was sifted, selected, structured and polished into novel-form.

The Project
Together, this novel, journal and notebook comprise the twenty-third installment in an ongoing novel-writing project in which the author is exploring the concept of form and meaning in the novel, and of the novel as a form of expression in the 21st Century. All of the published journals and notebooks are available for free at www.johnpassfield.ca.

About the Author

John Passfield was born in St. Thomas, Ontario, Canada, and continues to reside in Southern Ontario, near Cayuga, with his family. He is interested in exploring the development of the novel as an art-form, and has written over twenty novels, twenty planning notebooks and twenty journals in his search for a form for the poetic novel of our time.

Novels by John Passfield

Grave Song
The Agony of Robert Chisholm

Jumbo
P. T. Barnum's Greatest Creation

Pinafore Park
The Swan Boat Incident

Water Lane
The Pilgrimage of Christopher Marlowe

Rain of Fire
The Ordeal of Conductor Spettigue

Victoria Day
The Fabric of the Community

The Wright Brothers
Flight is Possible

Leni Riefenstahl
The Valley of the Shadow

Babe Ruth
Out of the Park

Raskolnikov
Murder with an Axe

Sergei Eisenstein
Death Day

Albert Einstein
Wonder

Geoffrey Chaucer
Canterbury Bound

Ospringe
A Visit with Grandad

Pompeii
Vesuvius Dominus

Beethoven
The Ninth Immersion

Job
The Cornerstone of the Universe

Bethune
The Only Person Alive in the World

Terry Fox
Somewhere the Hurting Must Stop

Lord and Lady Macbeth
Full of Scorpions Is My Mind

Cyril Passfield
Out West

Glenn Gould
Light and Dark

Emily Brontë
More Myself Than I

L. M. Montgomery
I Gave You Life

Pauline Johnson
Know Who I Am

See www.johnpassfield.ca for publishing information.

In Search of Form and Meaning:
Journals by John Passfield

Each journal is a day-by-day record of the complex process that a writer under-goes while crafting a work of art. It records the largest decisions, of structure and theme, and the smallest decisions, such as the choice of one word over another, and the constant interaction between the two. Each journal is a record of a writer's reflection on the craft of novel-writing.

The Making of Grave Song

The Making of Jumbo

The Making of Pinafore Park

The Making of Water Lane

The Making of Rain of Fire

The Making of Victoria Day

The Making of Flight is Possible

The Making of The Valley of the Shadow

The Making of Out of the Park

The Making of Murder with an Axe

The Making of Death Day

The Making of Wonder

The Making of Canterbury Bound

The Making of Ospringe

The Making of Vesuvius Dominus

The Making of The Ninth Immersion

The Making of The Cornerstone of the Universe

The Making of The Only Person Alive in the World

The Making of Somewhere the Hurting Must Stop

The Making of Full of Scorpions Is My Mind

The Making of Out West

The Making of Glenn Gould: Light and Dark

The Making of Emily Brontë: More Myself Than I

The Making of L. M. Montgomery: I Gave You Life

The Making of Pauline Johnson: Know Who I Am

See www.johnpassfield.ca for publishing information.

The Novel as an Art-Form:
Planning Notebooks by John Passfield

Each planning notebook is a printed version of the hand-written notebook which records the planning, writing, editing and polishing of each novel. Each notebook is an attempt to record, understand, and organize the vast cluster of thoughts which occur as one grapples with the various levels of organization which a clear yet complex work of art demands.

Planning Grave Song

Planning Jumbo

Planning Pinafore Park

Planning Water Lane

Planning Rain of Fire

Planning Victoria Day

Planning Flight is Possible

Planning The Valley of the Shadow

Planning Out of the Park

Planning Murder with an Axe

Planning Death Day

Planning Wonder

Planning Canterbury Bound

Planning Ospringe

Planning Vesuvius Dominus

Planning The Ninth Immersion

Planning The Cornerstone of the Universe

Planning The Only Person Alive in the World

Planning Somewhere the Hurting Must Stop

Planning Full of Scorpions Is My Mind

Planning Out West

Planning Glenn Gould: Light and Dark

Planning Emily Brontë: More Myself Than I

Planning L. M. Montgomery: I Gave You Life

Planning Pauline Johnson: Know Who I Am

See www.johnpassfield.ca for publishing information.